Harlequin ◆ Romances

OTHER
Harlequin Romances
by KAY THORPE

Many of these titles are available at your local bookseller
or through the Harlequin Reader Service.

For a free catalogue listing all available Harlequin Romances,
send your name and address to:

HARLEQUIN READER SERVICE,
M.P.O. Box 707, Niagara Falls, N.Y. 14302
Canadian address: Stratford, Ontario, Canada N5A 6W4

or use order coupon at back of books.

SAFARI SOUTH

by

KAY THORPE

Harlequin Books

TORONTO • LONDON • NEW YORK • AMSTERDAM • SYDNEY • WINNIPEG

Original hardcover edition published in 1976
by Mills & Boon Limited

ISBN 0-373-02046-5

Harlequin edition published February 1977

Printed in U.S.A.

CHAPTER ONE

'Odd how subconsciously you expect people to look exactly the way they did when you last met,' Keith remarked humorously when they had left the airport and were heading along the broad highway into Durban. 'That snap you sent with your last letter was almost a shock. In my mind's eye you were still seventeen and all gangling schoolgirl limbs, not at all a sophisticated young woman!'

Karen laughed, glancing her brother's way with an affection in no way tempered by the long parting now that they were together again. 'I don't feel at all sophisticated, and I'm sure I don't look it either. I'm not the type.'

'No, perhaps not,' with an oblique look at her finely moulded features beneath the shining cap of chestnut hair. 'Prettier even than I expected, though, and surprisingly self-possessed. I'm glad we didn't leave it any longer getting together again.'

'So am I.' Karen said it softly, thinking back to the day she had received the letter asking her to visit Keith and his wife here in Natal; the warmth of knowing he wanted to see her as much as she wanted to see him. In the four years since he had left England there had been comparatively little correspondence between them; it was only during the course of these last few months since her twenty-first birthday that they had begun to take up the relationship with any real meaning again.

Keith had been something of a surprise too. Not that his fair good looks had altered so radically from her memory of him. No, the difference was more intrinsic: a kind of overall maturity which gladdened her heart. He had always been such a restless personality, but at last he seemed to have settled down. This present job as manager of the Ryall plantation had already lasted eighteen months and seemed set to go on indefinitely.

Karen had been six and her brother just thirteen when their parents had died in a road accident, and she could scarcely remember them at all. She and Keith had been brought up by an aunt and uncle who had done all they could to make up for the tragic gap in their young lives, but Keith had always been the odd one out, too old, perhaps, to accept any substitute for the father he had idolised. At eighteen he had left home to share a flat with a couple of other youths of similar bent, flitting from job to job over the next two years as if unable to find his niche in the world, until the wanderlust had finally carried him off overseas to further the search.

He had been working for a firm of sugar exporters in the West Indies when he had met and married Denise. A short time afterwards the two of them had come over on a brief visit to England before taking off for South Africa, and that was the last Karen had seen of either of them until now.

'Denise would have come with me to meet you,' Keith said now, cutting in on her thoughts. 'But she thought we ought to have a little time on our own first. She's looking forward to seeing you again.'

Karen wondered if that were strictly true. Denise had evidenced little interest in her husband's young sister when they had been in England, and certainly none at all since. On the other hand, it was hardly to be expected that a seasoned young woman of twenty-three would have found very much in common with a seventeen-year-old who had never even been outside the British Isles. The difference in years was still the same of course, but the gap had to have narrowed somewhat. Denise probably realised that herself.

'Tell me about Breckonsridge,' she begged. 'All you said in your letter was that it's about eighty kilometres from the coast.'

'That's right. We cut inland just above Shakaskraal. If I put a spurt on we should make it before dark.' He paused musingly. 'What to tell you? It's one of the few privately owned sugar plantations still left in these parts, and Brad aims to keep it that way. We have a bungalow some short distance away from the main house, but we can use the pool any time we want to. A good deal of the time he's away looking after the rest of the Ryall interests, but right now he's home—although for how long is anybody's guess.'

'Does his wife always travel with him?'

'He isn't married. There's never been the woman yet who could hook Brad Ryall, and plenty have tried.'

'Doesn't he care for women very much?'

Keith laughed. 'He likes them all right. Just doesn't intend letting one tie him down before he's good and ready. Even then I imagine it will be more to keep the line going than through any yen for domesticity. He's been on his own long enough not to have any dire need of a wife to keep his household in order.'

Karen wrinkled her nose. 'He sounds charming!'

'He can be that too. One of those men who manage to get along equally well with both sexes. It's an enviable trait.'

She laughed. 'You seem to harbour quite an admiration for him yourself.'

'I suppose I do,' he returned equably. 'As bosses go he's a cut above average. Taking orders from a man only six years older than yourself could be a bit humiliating in some circumstances, but not with him. Most of the time I have a totally free hand.'

Providing he was running things exactly as required, Karen surmised. She had a feeling she wasn't going to like this Brad Ryall too much, despite Keith's enthusiastic build-up. Reading between the lines he sounded a mite too arrogantly sure of himself. Still, she was hardly likely to be having very much to do with him.

'What about you?' Keith asked now. 'Did they mind you coming out?'

The 'they' was both unfair and uncalled-for, but she chose to let it pass. 'Both Aunt Carol and Uncle Tom send their love,' she said mildly. 'No, of course they didn't object.

Why should they?'

'Because there's always the chance that you might want to stay once you've seen what it's like. Life out here is a whole lot different from what you're used to, Karen. There's room to breathe; room to spread. I wouldn't change it for a pension.'

Smiling, she said, 'I'm sure it's a great country, and I'm looking forward tremendously to seeing something of it, but this *is* just a holiday, Keith, while I'm in between jobs. Good thing I am, or I wouldn't have been able to come at all. No firm would have given me a whole six weeks off, just like that.'

'No, I guess not.' If he was disappointed by her reaction he didn't show it. Waving a hand at the wide, store-lined thoroughfare down which they were passing, he added, 'This is West Street, Durban's main shopping area. I'll take you along the Parade instead of cutting across Old Fort. It won't take much longer, and it may be a couple of weeks before we get into town again. Shall you mind being stuck so far out? We can't boast too much in the way of organised entertainment, although we do manage a reasonable social life.'

'Northampton isn't exactly the mecca of the jet set,' she responded on a light note. 'I'm used to a quiet life.'

'No boy-friends?'

'No one special.' It was true enough so far as it went. Colin had been good company, and she had been fond of him, but her heart had suffered no great blow when he had announced his engagement to another girl two months ago. All the same, she was thankful to have a good reason not to attend the wedding next month. The ex-girl-friend of the groom was always good material for malicious comment.

They had come out on to the sea-front now, the road wide and spacious, flanked by a sweeping frontage of modern hotel blocks on the one hand and with the foam-crested breakers of the Indian Ocean on the other. Karen gazed entranced at the Zulu rickshaw driver in his magnificent

8

horned headdress and beaded trappings loping easily along the far lane with his two passengers chatting easily behind. Commercialism perhaps, but nevertheless emotive. This was Africa, the Dark Continent, still but a hairsbreadth away from the days when the Zulus were a race of warriors living as their forebears had lived for centuries before them. Flying over it today and a great part of the previous night, Karen had felt dwarfed; an insignificant dot in all that immensity. She supposed a part of that reaction came from having lived all her life to date on a smallish island. It made for insularity in a way which could not be thrown off overnight.

It took five or six minutes to drive the whole length of the esplanade past sunken gardens and flower-strewn verges. Once out on the National Highway running northwards up the coast, Keith bade her look back for a view of the Durban skyline which made her catch her breath. Fronted by the blue and gold crescent of sand and sea, the piled structures of the city buildings looked like some vast modern sculpture, cunningly highlighted by the lowering sun.

'It's beautiful,' she said. 'But not the Africa I really came to see. Are there any townships close to Breckonsridge?'

'Colesburg is ten miles west of us. There's a sizeable hospital and a school, and a market on Saturdays. Then we have the club, of course. That's a must for a district like ours. Always something on at the weekends. Do you play tennis?'

'Some.'

'Breckonsridge has a court, too. Brad plays like a pro. Few of us are good enough to match him.'

Brad Ryall was beginning to irritate her even before she had met him. Karen hoped it would be some time before she did so. 'That lets me out,' she said without regret. 'My game is strictly amateur.'

'You'll not be short of partners whatever kind of game you play. Unattached females are in short enough supply to make you a star happening among the younger element in our circle.' Voice light enough to be taken jestingly, he added, 'Who knows, you might even find yourself a husband out here and then you wouldn't want to go back. After all, you don't want to be a secretary all your life.'

Karen said a trifle dryly, 'We do have men in England. Anyway, I don't want to marry anybody just yet, thanks. I enjoy earning my own living, and I'm good at my job.'

'You don't have a job right now.'

'I don't think I'll have any difficulty getting another. I was ready for a change, and your letter coming when it did seemed to make this as good a time as any. I haven't spent a great deal during these last three years so I can afford to indulge myself without feeling guilty about it, but I owe Aunt Carol and Uncle Tom a lot for all they've done for me. They've been as close to a real mother and father as they could be.'

'I don't doubt it. But as your real brother don't I have any claim on your loyalties?'

Karen bit her lip, not quite certain how to answer that question. Keith was her true next of kin, yes, but blood was not necessarily the binding factor in a relationship. Familiarity counted for a lot, and in many ways he was almost a stranger. She didn't understand this sudden desire of his to convince her into staying in South Africa permanently. He had a wife; why should he need a sister, now, after all these years?

'We have a lot of catching up to do,' she said at last. 'I'd have thought you'd want to wait and see how it goes yourself first, Keith.'

'You're right, of course.' His smile was wry. 'It was seeing you again that did it. It suddenly came over me how much we've missed out on. I wasn't allowing for your feelings.' The blue eyes, so like her own, flicked towards her and away again. 'All right, let's just leave things as they are for the present. You're here on holiday and that's all.' A moment later he added lightly, 'You must be tired after seventeen hours in the air. Why don't you take a nap? I'll wake you before we reach the estate.'

Karen was tired, and only just beginning to realise it, but she doubted that she would be able to sleep. Nevertheless she slid down a little in the leather seat and closed her eyes to rest them. The car, sleek and powerful, ate up the miles, lulling her despite herself. Everything about the vehicle shouted money. She wondered if it really belonged to Keith or went with the job. Either way, his use of it indicated a pretty good standard of living. He appeared to have fallen right on his feet with this job. Karen was glad for him—glad for Denise too. She could only hope that the Grainger fortunes would continue to flow as smoothly from here on in.

She must have dozed eventually, for when she opened her eyes again they were running between fields of cane higher than the car, their fan-like tops waving gently in the evening breeze. When Karen had thought about it at all she had imagined sugar cane to be planted in strictly regimented rows on the flatter areas of ground, but this was everywhere, following the contours of the countryside, filling the dips and rises with the same waving yellow-green as far as the eye could reach. The light was going fast, lending the distant mountains a purpling unreality. Once again she had that sense of vastness out there. It made her feel oddly lonely, despite Keith's presence at her side.

'Only a few minutes now,' he said as she sat up. 'I'm taking you in the back way to avoid going round by the house. You don't mind arriving by the tradesmen's entrance?'

Karen smiled, easing herself a little stiffly in the seat. 'I don't mind how I arrive providing I can have a sit-down somewhere stationary. It seems more like a week than a mere thirty hours or so since I set off from home. Is there any chance of a bath before dinner?'

'Sure. We have all the modern amenities. We're tapped into Colesburg's mains water supply, and electricity was laid on a few years back. Before that Breckonsridge had its own lighting plant. I'll get Aaron to run you one as soon as

11

we get in.'

'Aaron?'

'Our house-servant. His wife does the cooking. Between them they leave Denise very little to worry about.'

'Doesn't she find that rather boring?'

'I don't think so.' He sounded surprised. 'It's the accepted thing to have somebody in to take care of all the chores. Brad employs five or six to run his place.'

Karen could well believe it. No doubt that man didn't stir a muscle unless it was to further his own personal interests. With Keith to run Breckonsridge for him he could afford to sit back and take things easy.

Presently they turned in off the roadway beside a clump of mango trees and ran for a short distance along a lightly surfaced lane before coming to a stop in front of a compact bungalow. It was set within a small neat garden and had a red-tiled roof. More than that Karen could not ascertain in the swiftly encroaching darkness.

An African, middle-aged and sparely built, came down the porch steps as they approached the front entrance. He acknowledged Karen's greeting with grave courtesy, moving on down to the car to fetch her suitcases from the boot. Denise met them on the veranda, very little altered from the way Karen remembered her; tall and smoothly curved, the corn-coloured hair drawn up and back from her coolly lovely face. The smile on her lips didn't quite reach the hazel eyes, Karen noted, and the voice, though pleasant enough, held no true warmth.

'Nice to see you again after all this time. Did you have a good journey?'

Karen made the customary responses, and moved on with her to take in the welcoming comfort of the lounge immediately beyond the veranda. Chairs and chesterfield were in dark blue rep with multi-hued cushions scattered about them, and the curtains a paler shade of blue against almost identically coloured walls; the carpet was grey. To the rear was a roomy dining alcove containing a black-wood table and chairs, the former already set out for dinner with a striking arrangement of some scarlet blossom Karen did not recognise forming a centrepiece.

'How lovely!' she exclaimed impulsively. 'Did you do that yourself, Denise?'

The older girl made a small deprecating movement of her shoulders. 'I don't usually bother, but the occasion seemed to call for something.' There was a slight pause and a subtle alteration in tone as she added, 'Brad was down earlier, Keith. I invited him to dinner to meet Karen. He had nothing else arranged for tonight.'

Karen would have infinitely preferred to share her first meal in her brother's home with just the two of them, but even if it had not already been too late it was not her place to protest against the arrangements. That latter statement had only served to confirm her impressions of this Ryall man: having nothing else better to do he might just as well spend his evening vetting his manager's young relative. She had to meet him some time, she supposed, but she would rather it had waited a day or two.

Keith was studying his wife without expression. 'I'd have thought Brad would be the last to want to sit in on a family reunion.'

'Well, he's coming anyway.' Denise glanced back to Karen, face a shade tauter. 'I'll show you where you're sleeping. Aaron will have taken your bags through the back way.'

Karen went with her along a corridor with doors on both sides, and into a square bedroom furnished in a light wood not unlike teak. There were slatted blinds over the windows, and curtains in a gay cretonne. The cover on the single bed was a deep olive green picking out the motif in the carpet. Her suitcases stood ready and waiting at the bed end.

Denise stayed in the doorway as Karen moved forward to take the keys from her handbag and insert them in the lock. 'I'll leave you to it then. We eat at seven-thirty. There's no need to go to any trouble. Brad won't be expecting a formal occasion. The bathroom is two doors down

13

on this same side. Aaron will run you one if you sing out when you're ready.'

Karen said quickly, 'That's all right, I can do it myself.'

'Suit yourself.' The shrug was careless. 'See you later.'

Left alone, Karen opened the first suitcase and extracted the top few items to get down to her dresses, selecting a terra-cotta silk print with long full sleeves and a slim pleated skirt which the shop had assured her would pack like a dream. They had not lied. Hung up ready to slip into after she had had her bath, it displayed not a single crease.

There obviously wasn't going to be time to put everything away now. She contented herself with taking out only the items she was going to need immediately and left the rest for later.

The bathroom was tiled in green and white and displayed signs of fresh paint around the window where the plaster had apparently been recently renewed. In this climate maintenance was probably a full-time job in itself. Even now, in what amounted to early spring in this part of the world, the temperature was like that of a really good English summer, although it had cooled noticeably towards nightfall. Still warm enough to need only a light wrap outdoors, though.

Karen wondered if she would care for the summers out here. Keith had said in his letters that they were often stinking hot and humid. Not that it made any difference really. Denise, it was apparent, did not quite share her husband's enthusiasm over having her here as a guest, and would hardly be likely to want her on any permanent basis. Karen couldn't blame her, and yet, perversely, was beginning to wish it might have been possible. Having found Keith again she was going to hate losing him when the time came for her to return home. But that was a whole six weeks away yet. Silly to be thinking about leaving when she had only just got here.

Back in her room she got into the silk print and applied a trace of eye-shadow and lipstick, but left her skin unpowdered. The face looking back at her from the mirror was too familiar to be judged objectively. Keith had said she was pretty, which was something she had never considered herself—and still didn't, if it came to that. Colin, with his artist's eye, had always commented favourably on her bone structure and sketched her more than once, yet when it came to choosing his future wife had fallen for a blonde, blue-eyed, baby doll type girl who was the exact antithesis of everything he had ever claimed to admire in female beauty. It just went to show that love took little note of ideals.

Forgetting her looks, Karen ran a brush over her hair and got to her feet to step into a pair of slender-heeled sandals, sprayed herself lightly with toilet water and was ready to go.

She found the lounge empty when she went through. More lamps had been lit, affording a cosy glow she found vaguely reassuring. Aaron came in with a tray of drinks which he set ready on a side table. Smilingly, Karen declined his offer to prepare her one, preferring to wait until the others were here too.

There was a small stack of expensive glossy magazines in the rack close by the chesterfield. She chose one and was idly leafing through it when the car drew up outside. A door closed, and footsteps came up on to the veranda. Karen felt a swift instinctive tensing of nerve and sinew as a man wearing a light tropical lounge suit appeared in the open doorway, pausing there for a moment with one dark brow lifting in slow speculation as he met her widened blue eyes.

'Hallo,' he said, 'I appear to be early.'

Karen closed the magazine and took refuge in formality. 'I'm sure the others will be here shortly, Mr Ryall. I'm Keith's sister.'

'So I gathered.' He sounded faintly amused. 'Nice to meet you, Miss Grainger.' He came further into the room and dropped easily into the chair opposite, hitching his trousers to cross one knee comfortably over the other with an air of familiarity that was not lost on her. 'Keith get to

15

the airport in good time? We had a spot of trouble before he set off this morning. I was afraid it might have made him late.'

'He was there when I got in.' Karen wondered briefly what he meant by trouble but did not care to ask. She hoped either Keith or Denise would put in an appearance soon. What on earth did one talk about with a complete stranger?—especially one who was far more at home in this room than she was herself.

Aaron's return was a relief. 'Perhaps you'd like a drink?' she ventured, and saw the strong mouth take on a decided tilt.

'Thanks.' To the African he added pleasantly, 'The usual for me.' Grey eyes came back to where she sat. 'Aren't you going to join me?'

She started to shake her head, caught the satirical gleam and abruptly changed her mind. 'A small gin and tonic, please,' she told Aaron. 'With ice, if there is any.'

'That's one thing we never run short of.' Brad Ryall took out a cigarette case, leaning over it to offer it to her. 'Do you?'

Karen didn't very often, but she was not about to risk that jeering smile again. She took one of the long filter tips and put it to her lips, steeling herself as he got up and came across with a light. His hand was long and lean and powerful, the movement of thumb on lever decisive. Everything about the man was decisive, despite his casual manner. She was vitally aware of the masculinity in his strongly defined features and tall, leanly muscled frame. Something inside her tautened almost painfully, relaxing only when he had regained his seat.

There was an enigmatic smile on his lips as he lit his own cigarette. 'What's your impression of our part of the world up to now?' he asked negligently, slipping both lighter and case back into a pocket.

She answered in the same vein. 'I'll let you know when I've had time to form one.'

'Then we must do what we can to give you an overall

16

picture. Do you like riding?'

'Cars or horses?' she queried with deliberation, and drew a short laugh.

'Either, or both, if you like. There's a Marina in the garage you can have the use of if you want to get around on your own. Alternatively I have a nice little chestnut mare just about right for you.'

It was a moment before she answered. 'You're very generous.'

His glance was quizzical. 'Not what you expected?'

She warmed a little, conscious of being mocked. 'Why should I have decided what to expect of someone I'd never met?'

'Why indeed? I was going on the way you looked at me when I came in just now—as if I might have two heads. Or do you merely hold a grudge against the whole sex?'

'That's ridiculous!'

'Oh, I don't know. Stranger things have happened. A love affair gone wrong accounts for many a subsequent antagonism.' The mockery subtly increased. 'Ever been in love?'

Her chin lifted. 'Not that I can remember. How about you?'

The comeback had not been expected. Momentarily his brow quirked, then he lifted broad shoulders, mouth amused. 'Any number of times.'

'But never with any depth.'

'What makes you say that?'

The pause was brief. 'You're not married.'

'And you consider that the natural outcome of a love affair?'

She said calmly, 'I consider it the natural outcome of any real exchange of feeling between two people, but no doubt my idea of love differs considerably from yours.'

'No doubt.' His tone held irony. 'You're a romantic, young Grainger.'

'That's better than being a cynic.' The conversation was getting out of hand, but Karen refused to be the first one to

17

back out of it now. 'Most of us need some romance in our lives, but someone like you ...'

'Yes?' he prompted with interest as she broke off. 'Someone like me needs ... what?'

She caught her lip between her teeth, aware of having already said more than she intended. How had they managed to get on to such a subject in the first place? He hadn't been in the house more than ten minutes.

'I think you probably never allow your heart to rule your head,' she said slowly.

'Only probably? You disappoint me. I was beginning to think I'd at last discovered a female capable of sticking to a decision, right or wrong.'

Blue eyes registered the satire but did not flinch from his regard. 'I'd say recognition of one's own fallibility was the better quality.'

'Only for those who have no faith in themselves.' There was a tolerant note in his voice now, as though humouring a child. 'First impressions are usually fairly reliable providing one's perception hasn't become dulled through lack of use.'

Karen would have given a lot at that moment for the courage to ask what *his* first impressions of her might be, but she could imagine what he would make of any such show of interest. She wasn't at all certain herself why she should feel any concern whatsoever over what he thought about her. If a good impression had been her intention she would hardly have allowed herself to get involved in this discussion with her brother's employer.

And that latter fact was something she ought to bring herself to remember. She was a visitor here at Breckonsridge, and as such hardly in any position to start criticising the owner. She made a production of stubbing out the remains of the cigarette, carefully avoiding the gaze which had not left her face, and was infinitely grateful when Denise came into the room.

Brad got to his feet in one lithe movement to greet her, openly appreciating the combination of mid-blue dress and corn-silk hair. Denise's smile was quick and spontaneous, her voice holding a lilt which had been missing earlier.

'Sorry not to be here when you arrived, Brad. I didn't hear the car.'

'My fault. I was early.' His tone was easy. 'Your sister-in-law has been looking after me.'

'Oh?' Hazel eyes briefly flicked Karen's way, losing something of their animation in the process. 'Then I don't need to bother introducing you. Keith will be out in a moment. He couldn't find his cuff links.'

The mobile left eyebrow rose a fraction. 'He only has one pair?'

'No, but he naturally wanted the ones not immediately to hand.' She said it calmly enough, but with an underlying irritation which Karen, for one, noted. 'I hope you've been treating Karen kindly, Brad. She's new to all this.'

'I treat all lovely young things kindly.' The grey gaze came back to mock. 'No complaints, Miss Grainger—or may I call you Karen?'

'Please do,' she returned. 'And I'm sure you never have any complaints, Mr Ryall.'

'Brad.' That the dig had registered was apparent from the sudden glint in his eyes, but he let it go without retaliation. 'We don't go in for formality very much in these parts, as you'll find out for yourself before long. You must meet some people. I'll arrange a braii for this coming Saturday and get everyone over.'

She said swiftly, 'Thanks, but it isn't at all necessary to go to all that trouble.'

'Don't be ungrateful, darling,' put in Denise on a smooth note. 'The Breckonsridge braais are quite an event, and it's good of Brad to offer to put one on for your sake. If there's anything I can do, Brad ...' She let the offer trail away with a smile. 'Well, you know I'm always here.'

He was smiling back at her with the familiarity of long acquaintance. 'You can do the organising for me, if you will. Things always run smoothly when you're in charge,

19

Denise. It's an admirable quality in a woman—especially a wife.'

'It sure is,' Keith agreed lightly from the doorway. 'Everything go okay today, Brad?'

'We finished cutting the south patch. If this cool spell lasts a few days we should be well ahead of schedule.' He paused. 'By the way, I've paid off the two men you found fighting this morning. Seems they've been at each other's throats since you took them on. If they've got a beef, fair enough, but let them fight it out at somebody else's expense. That kind of thing disrupts the whole timetable.'

Keith was fixing himself a drink, seemingly unperturbed by the implied criticism. 'Might have a bit of a job finding replacements right away. I thought a warning might be sufficient.'

'Too risky. This time it was only fists, next time it might be knives. Get a warring element in a gang and it tends to rub off. If you can't find replacements we'll have to get along without them, that's all.'

But it would be Keith who answered if the cane didn't get cut on time, Karen surmised, and felt herself harden afresh towards the man sitting opposite. So far there was little sign of the charm Keith had spoken of—except for that glib compliment he had paid Denise a moment ago. In her eyes he was arrogant, mocking, and not a little despotic; hardly qualities to admire in a man. Yet she couldn't deny the quickening of her senses to his presence either. No woman with normal reflexes could fail to be aware of him, and Karen's reflexes were very normal indeed.

She had a vague premonition that it might have been better had they not been.

CHAPTER TWO

It was several days before Karen began to get her bearings around the Ryall plantation, to realise the extent of boundaries unmarked by fences or any other such instantly recognisable statement of ownership. The whole estate, she learned, ran to some four thousand acres of richly productive land, with maize and fruit forming substantial sidelines in addition to the main sugar crop.

Keith drove her out around the dirt tracks which bisected the fields, showing her the sugar being cut and trimmed and loaded on to the trucks which would take it down to the coast to be milled and converted into its various by-products. The hands chanted and sang as they worked, arms swinging rhythmically, demeanour unhurried in the pre-noon heat. Fire still smouldered in some cleared areas where the 'trash' had been burnt off ready for ploughing and replanting; in others a portion of stalk had been left from which another crop would grow—what Keith called 'ratooning'.

In all, he told her, they could gain three economical crops from each planting before starting over again, each crop taking roughly twenty months to reach maturity. It was a continuous process but not by any means a straight-forward one, disease, and cane pests like the moth borer taking their toll if not kept strictly in check.

The manager's bungalow lay some half a mile from the main house through a narrow belt of banana and peach trees forming part of the orchard. Karen saw the latter from the estate car Keith used for work on her second morning at Breckonsridge, a long low, white-walled structure comfortably sprawling amidst the prolific colour of its surround-

21

ing gardens. Of Brad Ryall himself she had seen or heard nothing since that first night, although she knew Denise had been over to the house regarding arrangements for the braai he had promised. Karen wished it had been possible to refuse the gesture, well-meant as it had apparently been. It placed her under something of an obligation to the man, and that was the last thing she wanted. She didn't try to question why.

Relations with her sister-in-law had neither improved nor deteriorated since her arrival. They lived in the same house, ate meals together, shared solitary hours when Keith was out, and yet they were still as far apart as two people could be. It wasn't dislike on Denise's part, Karen felt. More a total disinterest in her existence. She tolerated the visitor in her home, but that was as far as it went.

On one or two occasions Karen found herself wondering how Keith had managed to fall in love with someone who showed him so little outward affection. Denise was beautiful to look at but somehow almost untouchable. The only time she had seen her sparkle at all was when Brad Ryall had come to dinner.

A cold little hand enclosed her heart when she recalled that, but she refused to allow speculation any further rein. If Brad drew Denise's interest it could be because he was in himself an untouchable person, although in a different way. Had they both been free they might have suited one another admirably. Denise was the kind of wife a man like Brad needed: someone capable of fulfilling her role with smooth efficiency while making no untoward demands upon his emotions.

Friday was grey and overcast and cool. Towards teatime a wind sprang out of nowhere, mounting almost to gale force within the space of an hour or so and threatening to bring the orchard trees crashing to the ground. It was difficult to believe that this was the same country which only yesterday had basked beneath clear blue skies and sizzling sunshine, but assured by her brother that at this time of the year the weather could *and* would change again just as

22

dramatically, Karen could only sit back and wait for what the morning might bring. One thing was certain, if this continued the proposed luncheon party was off. She hardly knew whether to be glad or sorry at that particular prospect.

Keith was proved right, however, the day dawning fine and clear with a promise of heat to come. Denise disappeared after breakfast, leaving Karen to her own devices until Keith returned to the house at eleven. She didn't mind. It was pleasant to sit out on the veranda with a book and a cool drink in an atmosphere that vibrated with scent and sound, and not have to try to find ways of communicating with an unresponsive companion. She supposed the best thing was simply to stop trying, only that seemed so defeatist. Surely somewhere, somehow, she and Denise could find some point of common interest. If they couldn't the next few weeks were going to be rather difficult, not to say tension-fraught.

Keith looked hot and weary when he finally got back, his shirt sticking to his back. He slumped gratefully on the rattan couch with the long drink Karen had Aaron fetch for him, stretching out his booted feet to rest them on the rail.

'Trouble always comes in threes,' he said gloomily. 'One of the men slipped with a machete and nearly took his leg off a couple of hours ago. That leaves one more to go.'

'Is he going to be all right?' Karen asked.

'I'd say so. It's a bad gash, but we managed to stop the bleeding and patch him up well enough to get to the hospital. I had the foreman drive him in.' He finished his drink, added reluctantly, 'I suppose I'd better think about changing for this do over at the house. I met Brad on his way in half an hour ago, so at least I shan't have to play host.'

'He's been away?' queried Karen in some surprise, and drew a swift glance.

'Well, yes, didn't you know? He had to fly up to Jo'burg on Tuesday. I thought Denise had told you.'

'Perhaps she did and I wasn't listening properly.' Karen

knew that wasn't true, but there seemed little point in denying any attempt on her sister-in-law's part to tell her anything of the kind. Denise probably hadn't thought it necessary to pass on the news anyway. Why should she?

Tuesday. That meant Brad had left the very next day after her arrival. So he hadn't necessarily forgotten his offer to let her have use of the chestnut mare as she had imagined. Karen could not deny the small upward lift the news had given to her moral, although she had no real intention of taking him up on it should it be repeated now he was back, she told herself hastily. She wanted no part of Brad Ryall's careless generosity.

Keith still hadn't moved. He was gazing out over the wooden rail towards the belt of trees on the far side of the narrow lane, expression withdrawn. Looking at him, Karen wondered what he was thinking about right now, and wished she felt close enough to him to ask. That was the trouble, they never had been close the way brothers and sisters normally were. Even as children in their aunt's home they had lived their separate lives, though she supposed the gap in their ages accounted for a lot.

One thing was sure, he was not happy in the way she had thought him that first day. Settled here, yes, but not at rest within himself. Denise's fault? Karen couldn't honestly say. The relationship between the two seemed so flat—lifeless almost. Maybe all marriages declined somewhat after five years or so unless there were children to hold them together. Two people could become bored with each other, she imagined, although she couldn't see herself coming to feel that way about any man *she* had loved enough to want to marry in the first place.

'Do you ever regret leaving the West Indies?' she asked on a casual note, and he came back to earth with a faint start.

'What ... oh, sorry. I was miles away.' He shook his head. 'No, I don't regret it. Coming here gave me the kind of opportunity I'd been looking for. Short of owning my own place I couldn't be in a better position. You'd have to be born into a place like Breckonsridge anyway.'

'Does Denise feel the same way about it?'

An odd expression passed fleetingly over his face. 'She wouldn't live anywhere else. Jamaica held nothing for her. She needed a complete change of environment.'

She said softly, 'I wouldn't have thought this was so very different.'

'It is.' He made no attempt to add to that simple statement.

It was a moment or two before Karen could bring herself to ask the question she had been considering previously. 'Did you ever think of starting a family, Keith? This would be a children's paradise.'

Momentarily his mouth had tautened, then he relaxed and shrugged. 'Thinking about it isn't always enough. Anyway, kids are a bit of a liability.'

'But rewarding too, surely.'

He looked at her then, a brief glance which didn't really see her. 'We're not talking about the same things. Do you want to get ready first? We're due over there at twelve-thirty.'

The change of subject was too deliberate to be ignored. He was not prepared to discuss the matter. Karen made her way indoors feeling depressed and inadequate, aware that she had touched on a raw spot yet uncertain how to cope with that knowledge. Perhaps Denise couldn't have children. That would explain some part of Keith's reaction to her remarks. Yet if that were the case, surely his basic feelings for his wife should have managed to overcome bitterness—and it was that latter emotion which had been uppermost in his voice.

She was in her room before the logical alternative struck her, and it brought her up short. Supposing it was Keith himself who was unable to father a child? Such a situation could affect a man pretty badly, she imagined, especially if his wife proved herself lacking in the right kind of understanding. Karen hoped she was wrong but had an unhappy conviction that she had inadvertently hit the nail on the head. And if Denise couldn't find it in herself to support her husband through something like this, what chance did their marriage have of lasting out?

Relatively close as the main house was through the trees, it took a good five minutes to drive round by road. Passing through the wide ranch-style gateway into a gravelled court-yard, Karen saw they were not the first arrivals, three other cars already being parked along the far side of the extensive area. The sound of voices floated round from the rear of the house: somebody calling something and laughing, and the deeper boom of a man's tones answering.

Keith made, not for the big double doors which stood invitingly open to reveal a glimpse of a cool vestibule, but towards a wrought iron gate set in a tall hedge of blooming golden bignonia. They emerged on to a broad expanse of lawn running down a slight slope to the tree-sheltered pool. Several people already splashed in the dappled blue water, including a couple of children barely out of the toddler stage who were having the time of their lives scrambling up and down the corner ladder like agile monkeys.

The rear of the house was all covered terrace, the roof supported by white stone pillars. Chairs and loungers were scattered along the tiled length, while beyond french windows opened on a lounge of beautiful proportions. Karen had an impression of olive green and white decor with touches of purple and scarlet, then her whole attention was claimed by the man coming to greet them, her pulses responding without volition to the bronzed magnetism of muscular shoulders and hard-thewed legs.

Brad's thick dark hair was damp and slicked back, lending his features an angularity which emphasised the faint cynicism about his mouth. Karen felt his glance take in her simple yellow sundress and knew a momentary regret that she hadn't worn something a little classier, but his smile was reassuring.

'You seem to have adjusted nicely to the climate,' he said. 'I hope you brought a bathing suit. It's too hot to sit around in anything else.'

'I've got it on.' She suppressed an urge to grab hold of

Keith's arm as he started to move off in the direction of a couple lounging on the grass close to the pool. Don't leave me alone, she wanted to say. Clutching her raffia bag and not looking at the man in front of her, she said, 'Do we just throw our things over a chair, or what?'

'Not unless you want them sitting on,' he came back equably. 'There's a changing room at the end of the terrace with a plentiful supply of hangers. Pop along there before everybody starts arriving. We're going to be awash with bodies soon.' He turned his head to look towards the paved area beyond the pool where white-coated Africans were busily tending the preparation of a long table to receive the dishes no doubt already prepared inside the house in addition to the steaks and chicken joints stacked ready for the charcoal grills. 'I'd better go and yank Denise out of the kitchen. She's done a marvellous job getting the show on the road, but I didn't intend to encroach on her time to this extent. Especially with a visitor to take care of.'

'I'm sure she's thoroughly enjoyed doing it,' Karen responded quickly. 'And I've had plenty to do and see. Keith took me round the estate with him on Wednesday.'

'He did?' His smile was lazy, voice tolerant. 'And what was your impression of life on a sugar plantation?'

'Fascinating.' Blue eyes held a spark of defiance. 'Like being transported back in time. I imagine conditions haven't altered very much in the last hundred years.'

'With regard to the actual cutting, probably not.' The tolerance had gone from his voice and his smile was edged. 'The terrain here doesn't allow for mechanisation to any great extent. Keith obviously didn't carry your education quite far enough. We'll have to do something about that.'

It was too late to start apologising for the implication. Karen recognised that much, yet still felt bound to make some attempt. 'I didn't mean it quite that way,' she said, and saw his lips twist.

'I think you did, but I'll give you the benefit of the doubt. I'm sorry I haven't been available to show you round the place myself these last few days. I'll make amends

27

starting tomorrow. Have you made friends with Rennie yet?'

'Rennie?'

'The mare I said you could use. I asked Denise to bring you over with her.'

'Oh, that.' She avoided his eyes. 'I preferred to wait till you got back. I'm not a very good rider ... at least, not very experienced.'

'Then now's an ideal opportunity to put in some practice. I'll expect you at ten. Take the Marina when you go, then you can drive round.' He paused, brows lifting quizzically. 'You *do* drive?'

'Yes.' She wanted to refuse but couldn't find the words. 'Thank you,' she tagged on somewhat grudgingly, and drew the cynical smile again.

'That's all right. No strings attached. Cut along and have a swim while the pool's still fairly quiet.'

Karen went before she could say something she might later regret. It was difficult to meet Brad Ryall on equal terms. He had a way of placing one at a disadvantage without even trying. Yet that same quality had an oddly stimulating effect. She had never felt quite so alive as she did at this moment feeling the grey eyes following her as she made her way on to the terrace.

People arrived in droves over the next half hour, the majority dressed casually and comfortably in shorts and a variety of tops. Several brought children with them, the latter losing no time in joining the two already in the pool. Laughter filled the air, rising above the music filtering out from the lounge.

Karen took a dip herself before they ate, squeezing out her hair and leaving it to dry naturally in the sun as she joined the crowd around the long table. Brad had introduced her to one or two couples and then left her to make her own way. With folk like these it wasn't at all difficult. Everyone knew everyone else, and they accepted her into their midst with heartwarming eagerness to make her feel completely at home.

'We're only first generation South Africans ourselves,' the mother of the two children who had been here on her arrival told her. 'Both my parents and my husband's originated from Scotland. You'll find a great many people here have roots in Britain, although we have a lot of German and French blood too, as well as the Dutch. A very mixed bag when you think about it.'

But well adjusted, Karen thought. These people had a style that was all their own. She liked it; she liked them. She could begin to understand now why Keith wanted to stay.

Denise was the only one who didn't seem to fit. Smiling, chatting in apparently casual fashion with these neighbours she must have known for at least a year, she still managed to hold herself aloof. She was about the only woman wearing a dress, her blonde hair smooth and immaculate, make-up unflawed. Mistress of the manor, Karen reflected without amusement, and wondered if she were on her own in noting the proprietorial air with which her sister-in-law dished out instructions to the servants. Certainly if Brad himself noticed he didn't appear to be minding, despite what he had said earlier.

She was sitting on the side of the pool watching the children still at play in the water when the latter finally sought her out again. He had changed from the white trunks into shorts and a cotton shirt; the dark hair was rough and slightly wavy at the ends, as if he had simply run a hand through it.

'Just to have that amount of energy!' he commented lightly, dropping to a seat beside her on the grass. 'They've been at it for a couple of hours now. Thinking of going in again yourself?'

Karen shook her head, drawing up her knees to hug her chest in a gesture any psychologist would have interpreted as self-protective. 'I've had enough for one day. Do you use the pool on your own very much?'

'Most mornings when I'm here.'

She cast him an oblique glance which took in the firmness of his profile against the light slanting through the trees. 'Keith said you did a lot of travelling.'

'Too much. But all of it is necessary, I'm afraid.'

'Why?'

There was a pause, then he laughed. 'A good question. Maybe because I don't trust anyone else to see to things for me.'

'You leave Keith in charge here.'

'That's different.'

'Because he simply has to carry out your orders in your absence?'

'If you want to see it that way.' His voice had cooled. 'You know, you're not unlike him, except that he's had time to learn diplomacy. Anything else you'd like to clarifying?'

She flushed, conscious of having annoyed him—or perhaps irritated would be a better word. 'I'm sorry if I sounded critical.'

'No, you're not. You'd formed an opinion of me before you arrived and you're determined not to change it. Mules are stubborn that way too.'

'I believe you said the other night that first impressions were usually the best ones,' she retorted shortly.

'Provided they're gained without bias. Try crediting your brother with enough self-interest to smooth his own path. He wouldn't thank you for taking up cudgels on his behalf.'

Karen could imagine not. Impossible to explain that such had not really been her intention because that would call for reasons she was not prepared to go into. Sufficient to admit to herself that getting at Brad in this manner was more in the nature of a barricade than an attack. He had to be kept at arm's length.

'I'll try to remember,' she said. 'You probably know him better than I do.'

'I'd say definitely,' on a dry note. 'He's a man, and you don't appear to have too much understanding of the sex as a whole. That's something else I might just take it on myself

30

to teach you while you're here.'

'Don't bother. I've managed to get along so far.'

'More by good luck than good management, I'd imagine. You don't just ask for trouble, you sit up and beg for it.' His voice had regained its customary mockery. 'Next time you might be in for a surprise, young Karen!'

'Don't patronise,' she came back with what satire of her own she could muster. 'I'm neither that young nor that stupid, though I daresay you'd like me to be. What would you do, put me across your knee?'

His grin was sudden and unexpected. 'It's an idea worth bearing in mind.' There was a small silence. When he spoke again it was without the taunt. 'You may as well meet Rennie while you're here. Get some clothes on and come along to the stables. I'll wait for you on the path.'

Karen capitulated without thinking about it, suddenly uncaring of anything beyond the knowledge that she wanted to go with him. Caution was for the cautious, and they never got anywhere worth going.

She knew other eyes watched them as he lent her a hand to get to her feet, but she refused to let it make her self-conscious with him. No doubt any female in whom the district's most eligible bachelor took the remotest interest would be the subject of speculative comment. Only where she was concerned they would be wasting their time. Brad felt an obligation to see that his manager's sister enjoyed her stay on the plantation, and that was all there was to it. Well, not *quite* all, perhaps. Because she was so new to this kind of life it amused him to taunt her, to draw her out of her British shell of reserve and make her respond to him. Once he realised the limitations of her ability to keep the game going he would soon lose interest.

The stables were out of sight of the house close to the fringe of the orchards. Brad kept two animals, one the slender-legged chestnut he had offered Karen, the other a restless grey with a beautiful head.

'He has Arab blood,' Brad told her, rubbing the velvety nose pressed over the rail of the loose-box at him. 'I had

31

him shipped from the States the last time I was over. His name's Caliph. Come and say Hallo.'

She laughed and shook her head. 'I'll say it from here, thanks. He's got a wicked gleam in his eye.'

'He senses uncertainty, and any animal will take advantage of that if it can.' His tone was bland. 'It's up to you to prove you can better him.'

'Perhaps I could start with something easier and work up to it,' she suggested, and turned back to the chestnut on his derisive grin. 'She's a beauty. How long have you had her?'

'A couple of years. She's a good smooth ride.' He came up behind her, standing close enough for her to feel the faint stirring of his breath on the crown of her head. 'Not exciting enough for some, maybe, but capricious enough when the fancy takes her.' The pause held deliberation. 'How much riding have you actually done?'

'Just a little ordinary hacking. There's a stables quite close to home.' She wanted to move away from him, but that would be too much like admitting his power to disturb her. She kept her gaze fixed on the mare. 'I never had any proper lessons, I'm afraid, so I'll probably do everything wrong.'

'Your instincts seem pretty sharp.' He sounded amused. 'The technique isn't so important providing the rapport is there. Ever been thrown?'

'No.' Her heart was beating fast, her every sense alive to his closeness. 'I was told always to keep the rein tight.'

His laugh was low and appreciative. 'Good advice. Just keep remembering that and you won't go far wrong.' He moved forward into her line of vision, resting an arm along the top rail as the mare went back to her hay-net, mouth still curved in the smile which had been in his voice. 'Keith said you left your job to take this holiday. Weren't you happy where you were?'

Leaning back against the side support, Karen twirled a length of straw between her fingers and tried to match his ease of manner. 'It wasn't so much unhappiness as just plain boredom. Keith asking me to come out here provided the incentive I needed to make the decision to leave.'

'You prefer a challenge.'

'I think so. There's more to a good secretary than being proficient at typing and filing and making coffee. At college we were taught to take over all the day-to-day problems of running a business—something like an office wife, in fact.'

'That could have its moments.'

She glanced at him swiftly, felt her own lips curve in response. 'I'm sure they didn't mean it to be taken that seriously. Anyway, my boss was very happily married with a grown-up family.'

'And dull?' he suggested. 'Like the job. Next time you'll have to look out for a boss you can fall in love with. It might make life more interesting.'

'I'd say disastrous ... unless it were mutual.'

'Not desirable in business interests. Mind you, a man might do worse than marry his secretary. At the very least he'd get all his letters typed for free.'

Voice casual, she said, 'Surely a man wants more than efficiency in a wife. You make the whole thing sound like a business arrangement.'

'From what I've seen of some marriages that could have formed a better basis,' on a dry note. 'Love puts blinkers on a relationship. Compatibility comes first in my book. Once married there's nothing to stop a couple from falling in love.'

'Though not necessarily with each other.'

His gaze sharpened. 'That kind of cynicism doesn't suit you.'

'How many kinds are there?' She caught his eye and looked away again quickly, cheeks warming. 'It must be catching.'

'I'm twelve years older than you and through the rosy-hued stage,' he came back crisply. 'You haven't even had time to be disillusioned yet.'

'I've had time to realise that if two people love one another enough they can overcome a lot of difficulties.' Her

33

voice was low. 'It's when the feeling is unequal that problems mount.'

Something in the atmosphere had changed subtly in the last moment or two; Karen could feel the difference like something tangible.

'You've been here less than a week,' he said at last. 'Do you think that's long enough to reach any conclusions about people you haven't seen for years?'

'I don't know whether it's long enough, I just know there's something wrong.' She made herself meet his eyes. 'Keith and Denise were compatible, but it doesn't seen to have been enough in their case.'

'How would you define compatibility?' he asked on an odd note.

She hesitated. 'Well, having the same tastes, for one thing; sharing interests and ambitions.'

'No differences at all? No allowance for individualism?'

She frowned a little. 'Isn't that what you were saying?'

'No, it wasn't.' He studied her a moment, expression faintly ironical. 'My own fault for expecting too much. Your brother and his wife will work out their own solutions in their own good time. What they don't need is any kind of side-taking.'

In some way she had disappointed him. Karen dared not allow herself to care too much. 'Then there are sides to take?' she said.

'There are always sides to take, but anyone with a grain of sense stays impartial.' Impatience tinged his voice. 'Keep out of it, Karen. You don't know anything about these things.'

'He's my brother.' She was trembling and trying not to show it. 'Perhaps you find it easy to stand back and see someone you care for unhappy ... although as you obviously don't give a fig for anyone but yourself I suppose it would be. I imagine ...'

'I'd leave it right there if I were you.' He hadn't raised his voice, but the inflection was more than sufficient to pull her up short. His mouth was set, face hard. 'When I need a character reference I'll ask for it!'

She had already gone over the top, there seemed no point in backing off now. 'You can't expect to dish out criticism without getting it back,' she said huskily. 'Impartiality can be taken too far.'

'Not in a case like this.' He paused, then made an abrupt movement away from the rail to take her by the arm and swing her round to face him. 'Karen, I'm asking you to trust my judgment. Can't you even try?'

'Because you're older than I am?'

He sighed suddenly. 'No, because I happen to be in a better position, that's all.'

She gazed at him for a long moment, feeling the pressure of his fingers on her skin with a strange sense of detachment. 'You know what it's all about, don't you?' she said. 'You know what's wrong between them.'

'So I know. What I said still goes.'

'I might understand better if I knew too.' She saw his lips start to form the flat refusal and sought for a means of persuading him to change his mind. 'Brad, I have to live in the same house. Perhaps you're right in saying no one else can help, but at least I could be sure of not aggravating the situation any further.' She paused. 'It has something to do with them not having any family yet, doesn't it?'

Grey eyes narrowed. 'Is that guesswork, or something you overheard?'

'Guesswork. I could scarcely eavesdrop on nothing.'

'What's that supposed to mean?'

'It means that they don't have an awful lot to say to one another.'

The hand fell away from her arm and was pushed into a pocket. 'I know a hotel manager who swears he can always tell the married couples by the lack of conversation.'

Body tensed, she said, 'That's not funny.'

'It wasn't meant to be. Just an observation.' He studied her briefly, then shrugged. 'You want it in a nutshell. So be it. Keith wants children and Denise doesn't. It's as simple as that. Now let's drop it.'

35

'Simple!' She was too shaken to heed that last clipped request. 'How can you possibly write it off like that? It's what marriage is all about.'

'Procreation of the species?' His mouth twisted. 'I'd say we'd done more than enough already, judging by population figures. Women who feel the way Denise does are one of Nature's ways of equalling the balance, although she's falling pretty far behind.'

'What you're really saying is you're on Denise's side.'

'I already told you I don't take sides. I can understand the way she feels; I can understand the way Keith feels too. It's a hell of a situation because there's no adequate solution. Certainly none an idealist could provide.'

She said stiffly, 'You make it sound a crime to have ideals.'

'Do I?' He was smiling, but without humour. 'Perhaps I just don't see you finding anyone to live up to them. We'd better be getting back before people start leaving.'

Whatever rapport they had managed to achieve earlier it was certainly missing as they retraced their steps to the house. The couple with the two youngsters had them dressed ready to go and were already taking their leave of others nearby.

'I was beginning to think we'd have to run without thanking you for the braai, Brad,' said Molly Gordon, casting a swift glance towards Karen. 'Sorry we have to dash off, but we've got some people coming over later ourselves. It's been grand. The kids have had a whale of a time!'

'Molly was saying she'd heard the Harlows are coming back at last,' one of the other women commented when the Gordons had gone. 'Had you heard about it, Brad?'

'They're already in the country,' he said. 'I was with them in Jo'burg yesterday.'

'And they intend to run the farm themselves from now on?'

'Not exactly. They neither of them know enough about farming to risk getting rid of Ron Trent.'

'Then why *are* they coming back? It must be almost five years.'

'Neil thought it time he checked on his assets. Lowlands was home to him and Serena for twenty years before they went to the States. It's natural they should take a yen to see it again.'

'Are those two changed much?' asked one of the men with a grin. 'From what I remember, old Reg Harlow never had much control over either of them after their mother died. You'd have thought the girl would have quietened down quicker than the boy, even though they were twins, but to my reckoning she was the leader of the two.'

Brad's answering smile was perfunctory. 'They're twenty-five. You're bound to find them changed. Anyway, they're due to arrive in a couple of days. You can judge for yourself.'

'Did you get time to look round Jo'burg on your way down, Karen?' queried the woman who had first spoken.

Regretfully she shook her head. 'I only had a matter of an hour or so between planes. I might manage a couple of days on the way back.'

Out of the corner of her eye she saw Brad move to speak with some others who had just come up, and found herself conjecturing over these Harlow twins in whom everyone seemed so interested. Five years away, and yet he had travelled six hundred miles to spend a few days with them in Johannesburg. Tribute to old family friendship—or something more than that? Not that it made any difference either way.

With determination she brought her mind to bear on present company, smilingly responding to an invitation for the following week. Everyone was doing their level best to make this holiday enjoyable; already she had more invitations than she was probably going to be able to cope with in the time. It was going to leave little opportunity for despondency in any shape or form.

CHAPTER THREE

THE Grainger family was ready to leave before Brad mentioned the Marina again.

'You two go on,' he said to Keith. 'Karen can follow you down once I've shown her the controls.' To Denise he added, 'I hope to be able to repay you in part for all the work you put in to make today a success later on. My staff are never so well organised as when you're in charge.'

To Karen's ears there might have been an element of irony in that latter statement, but Denise appeared to take it at face value. She looked gratified and a trifle smug, hazel eyes smiling up into his. 'They're efficient, but inclined to laze if not gingered up. You should be more demanding with them.'

'Maybe you're right.' His tone was pleasantly noncommittal. 'You'll not mind eating at the club tonight? I've booked a table.'

'I'm looking forward to it.' She hesitated. 'Is it to be a private party?'

'At dinner, yes, although we'll no doubt get drawn into the general throng later. You know how these affairs tend to go.' He closed the door and smiled down at her, then turned to look at Karen with suddenly cynical eyes. 'Now to fix you up.'

The garage was enormous, housing three vehicles already and with room for another if necessary. Eyeing the bright yellow coupé which was to be her responsibility from now on, Karen could not deny a stirring of anticipation. She liked driving, and had done as much as she could since taking her test two years ago. Colin had driven a Ford Capri which she had found easy enough to handle. She imagined the Marina to be similar in performance. All the same, she still didn't care for the idea of taking it.

'It's this year's model,' she said. 'Supposing I damage it?'

'It's insured. And the thing to concentrate on is not damaging yourself.' The jeer was faint but unmistakable. 'If you're doubtful of your ability to handle it we'd better take a test run. You brought an international licence, of course.'

To deny it would solve the whole problem, she realised, and yet it seemed ridiculous to go to that much trouble to cut herself off from Brad's generosity. The car would enable her to move around on her own when she felt like it, to visit all the people who had asked her over without having to rely on Keith being available to run her about. The only real alternative was to hire one, and apart from not being able to afford to do that, she could imagine Brad's reaction to such an obvious snub. No, like it or not, she was committed.

'Yes,' she said.

'Then get in and show me what you can do.'

Surprisingly the challenge put her on her mettle. She slid behind the wheel without another word of protest, feeling her stomach muscles knot as he eased himself in beside her. Switching on the ignition, she thought resolutely, To hell with him! Either she proved her capabilities now or not at all. She liked driving, she knew she drove well, so why let him put her off. She would show him what she could do all right!

The main entrance to the estate was less than a quarter of a mile away. By the time they reached it, Karen had the feel of the vehicle and felt confident enough to put her foot down, thrilling to the surge of power from the supercharged engine. Overhead the sky was a canopy of blue, the sun a glowing beacon extending light and heat to a landscape not yet familiar enough to have become in any way commonplace. The trees lining the road were green with new spring growth, wild flowers gleaming among the dark foliage of the undergrowth. Every bend brought fresh vistas of undulating countryside, gentle, yet somehow still untamed. Heat haze shimmered over the tarmac ahead.

'Take it easy,' Brad admonished dryly after several kilo-metres had flashed by. 'We have restrictions over here too, you know.'

She eased off reluctantly, aware that she had nowhere reached the limit of the car's capabilities. 'It's such a temp-tation,' she said. 'All this empty road. Is it always so quiet out here?'

'Mostly. We're a bit off the beaten track.' He was sitting sideways in his seat, one arm resting along the open win-dow frame, the smile curving his lips not yet quite friendly again. 'Got it out of your system, or are you likely to shoot off like a rocket again on the first wrong word?'

She glanced at him swiftly and with some chagrin. 'You shouldn't have made it so obvious I was on probation. You offered me the car, I didn't ask.'

'Agreed, but you seemed sufficiently unsure of yourself to cast doubts on your experience. Who taught you?'

'Uncle Tom bought me a course of lessons for my nine-teenth birthday. My instructor said I was a natural.' She kept her voice light. 'I understand women drivers tend to be either very good or very bad: there's no in-between. Would you agree?'

'Mostly I'd say that women and driving were like oil and water. You might be a rare exception, providing you learn to curb that reckless streak. One of these days it could land you in a heap of trouble.'

'Are we still talking about cars?' she queried innocently.

His laugh held some slight reluctance. 'Cars, or anything else. You're an odd mixture, young Grainger. One minute the little hothead, the next as cool as they come!'

'Stand up, the real Karen Grainger.' There was some-thing about the feel of the wheel beneath her hands that gave her a totally new kind of confidence—perhaps the knowledge that for the moment she was in control. 'I'd be grateful if you'd stop calling me that. Back home twenty-one is considered reasonably mature. I've had the vote three years already.'

'I hope you made good use of it. And who told you maturity had anything to do with age?'

'It has to have *something* to do with it. One could scarcely be mature at ten.'

'One could be given a shove in the right direction,' dryly. 'You're coming along, but you've still got some way to go yet.'

'Like learning to settle for less than the best?' she couldn't resist asking. 'That's not maturity, it's defeatism!'

'Realism would be closer the mark if we're going to be pedantic. And if we're going to argue stop the car and let me have the wheel. The male of the species has an infinitely greater capacity for division of interests.'

'Plus an inflated ego to match.'

'You could be right. Self-criticism never did anything for anybody. Draw in round the bend here. I'll take us back.'

Karen obeyed with a smile playing about her lips, knowing he was doing it on purpose and determined not to rise to the challenge. 'It's your car.'

'Only when I'm in it.' He came round the bonnet and took her place as she slid over. 'Lesson number one on how to handle the male egotist: never appear to believe yourself his equal. We're most of us peacocks, honey, and the plumage doesn't stand too much ruffling.'

'So I'm beginning to learn.' There was stimulation in this kind of exchange. Danger too, she acknowledged on a faint quiver of apprehension—or was it anticipation? Either way, she was enjoying herself and didn't want to stop.

They were almost back at the house before he mentioned the evening.

'One of the few occasions when anyone bothers to dress up,' he said. 'Where the men are concerned, at any rate. You might call it a gala night.'

'Celebrating anything in particular?' she asked.

He shrugged. 'Some obscure local event. Nothing I can even remember. The reason is unimportant providing it gives some excuse. Out here we take full advantage of every possible one.'

41

'But you're not so far away from Durban that you couldn't at a pinch take advantage of real night-life,' Karen mused almost to herself, and drew a swift glance.

'Does that mean you're already hankering after the bright lights yourself?'

'No, it doesn't,' she returned without haste. 'It was just an observation. In six weeks I'm sure I'll find more than enough variety in entertainment around Colesburg.'

He was silent for a moment before saying evenly, 'You don't have any intention of extending your time beyond that then?'

'Well, no.' She was nonplussed. 'Hardly. Most people would think themselves more than fortunate to get that long a holiday.'

'You aren't most people, and your circumstances are rather different from the average holidaymaker.' He paused. 'You know Keith would like you to stay.'

It was a statement, not a question. Karen accepted it as such, frowning a little into the middle distance. 'Even if it were possible I couldn't.'

'That's a contradiction of terms. What you really mean is you wouldn't.'

'Now who's being pedantic?'

'Don't try changing the subject. Keith is your brother. Don't you think you owe him some family loyalty?'

'He's the brother I'm only just beginning to get to know again,' she pointed out after a moment. 'And I have other family back home.'

'They've had you most of your life, apparently. Keith needs you now.'

'That's not what you said earlier.'

'We weren't discussing the same thing, then. Now that you're here I think you should stay. I'd see to it that you didn't have any difficulty over the legal aspect.'

'It isn't as simple as that,' she came back a little desperately. 'I have other obligations apart from Keith. In any case, I'd have thought any permanent arrangement could only worsen the situation between him and Denise. It isn't even as though she and I ...' She broke off abruptly, aware of his sharpened regard.

'As though she and you ... what? Get along as sisters-in-law should? Few do. I wasn't suggesting you should make your home with them. Jobs in the area are scarce anyway ... the kind you'd be looking for.'

'Durban, of course. You could live in town and come out here at the weekends. There are plenty of people I could introduce you to down there.'

Karen looked at him for a long moment, unable to fathom the thoughts behind the unrevealing features. 'You must think a lot of Keith to go to all this trouble,' she said at last.

'He's a good man. The best manager I ever had. I'd like to know he had reason to stick around.' His mouth twisted. 'Motives are rarely altruistic, blue eyes.' He was drawing up in front of the house gates as he spoke, leaving the engine running as he opened the door. 'She's all yours from now on. See you later.'

He was gone before she could make any further comment, striding off towards the house without a backward glance and leaving her to slide back behind the wheel with a feeling that too many questions remained unanswered—and deliberately. She could see no possible way in which it could make any difference to Keith's place here whether she herself went or stayed in five weeks' time.

Denise was in the lounge when she reached the bungalow. As Karen entered the room she bent to stub out a cigarette into the already overflowing tray, straightening again with an oddly jerky movement as if she found difficulty in containing herself.

'Keith had to go out,' she said. 'Do you want some tea?'

'I'd love it.' Karen slid into a chair, no more at ease than she ever was with her brother's wife but willing to make the effort. 'Sorry if I've kept you waiting. Brad decided to give me a test drive while he was about it and we went rather further than we intended.'

'I doubt it.' Denise's smile was thin, her eyes lit with a kind of feverish brilliance. 'Brad decides exactly how far he

43

wants to go ... with everyone. Don't run away with the idea that you're going to be anything but a passing interest where he's concerned. When he takes a wife it's going to have to be one used to his kind of life in every respect, and you could hardly call yourself an adequate candidate.'

The attack, so totally unanticipated, left Karen blank for a moment. She gazed at the older girl speechlessly, unable to quite take in the implications. When she finally found her voice she was still uncertain of what she was going to say.

'Isn't that jumping a little far ahead?' she asked. 'I only met him for the second time today.'

'Once is usually enough for a woman to know when a man is worth having.' The glitter had not decreased in any way, and the fingers lighting yet another cigarette were unsteady. 'Brad is the best catch this side of Durban: he knows it, and so does everyone else. He's too used to being chased by women to be taken in by the kind of tactics you've been using. His lending you the car doesn't mean a thing. He'd have done it for anyone. And the braai was just an excuse ...' She broke off, took a quick pull at the cigarette and seemed to find some measure of calming influence in the act. 'That isn't important. I simply thought you ought to be warned not to bother wasting your time, that's all.'

'Thanks.' Karen couldn't quite keep the irony from her voice. 'I appreciate your concern. I suppose it's no use my denying having thought about him that way?'

'You can deny it, I don't have to believe it.' Denise got to her feet and walked over to the door, called 'Tea, Aaron!' with unwonted sharpness, and came back to resume her seat, flicking ash into the tray without bothering to look. 'How much did Keith tell you about the set-up here when he wrote to you?'

'Not a great deal.' Karen was hesitant, not sure what the other was getting at. 'I knew he was managing a sugar plantation, its name and approximate location. That's about all.'

'But obviously enough to bring you out here hot-foot, and just when Brad happens to be at home too. That has to be more than coincidence!'

Karen made no answer because there seemed none worth making. Whatever she said she obviously was not going to be believed. The whole thing was ludicrous, of course. She hadn't even known of Brad's existence before coming to South Africa. He had been a shadowy figure in her imagination: her brother's employer. In many ways she was beginning to wish he had remained so.

Aaron brought in the tea, his presence affording a slight lessening of the tension in the room. If he was aware of the atmosphere between the two women he gave no sign of it, features impassive as he set down the tray. Karen wondered how much of the conversation he had heard, and what he would have made of it. Denise had certainly made no attempt to keep her voice down.

She stole a glance at her sister-in-law when he had gone, to find her looking rather less on edge than she had been a few minutes ago, the cigarette no longer describing the frantic arc which had kept the end constantly aglow. Even so, there seemed quite a gap between her present state and the picture of cool composure she had hitherto presented. And it had been Brad who had sparked off the change in her—or more precisely, his actions this afternoon. Karen felt cold and raw. One didn't need to be anything of an analyst to realise why: jealousy was recognisable in most forms. And where did that leave Keith?

'Perhaps you'd prefer it if I made an excuse not to come with you to the club tonight,' she said after what seemed like an age of silence. 'I could always say I have a headache.' It wouldn't be much of a lie either, she thought painfully.

'The table is booked for four.' Denise's tone was short but lacking its former vehemence. 'Brad could scarcely do other than invite you to join us, but it might be better if you find some other engagement in future.'

That sounded as though invitations from the plantation boss were not an unusual occurrence. All of them including Keith? she wondered fleetingly, and felt a quiver of some emotion she didn't want to examine too closely run through her before she blanked off that trend of thought. She was getting ahead of herself, filling in details which didn't even exist. At least, she hoped they didn't.

Having said all she apparently intended to say for the moment on the subject, Denise made no further attempt at conversation of any kind. Karen drank the tea without tasting it, and escaped to the privacy of her own room as soon as she could, standing at the window to view the distant mountains with a feeling that the situation here was going to get worse before it got better—if it ever did get better. How long had Denise felt this way about Brad? And had he encouraged her? The relationship between the two of them seemed casual enough on the surface, but who could tell what went on behind those grey eyes? Certainly he admired his manager's wife, was in sympathy with her.

Her thoughts were going around in circles, she acknowledged wearily, and without further proof no conclusions could be reached either way. Her main concern had to be with Keith. Obviously he didn't suspect anything between his wife and his employer or he would hardly still be working for the latter.

One thing all this did explain was Denise's reluctance to start a family. Few women could probably contemplate having a child by one man while yearning for another. If only they had never come to Breckonsridge at all, never met up with Brad Ryall. Perhaps their marriage had not been perfect before, but at least it might have stood a chance. What chance did it have now?

Keith didn't return to the house until almost six o'clock. Karen heard the car from her bedroom, but she did not go out to greet him, afraid he might sense something odd in her manner. Brad was to pick them all up at seven-thirty. Getting into a turquoise cotton with narrow shoulder straps and a matching stole, she willed herself to a state of personal detachment over the coming evening. At all costs Keith must be kept from guessing Denise's feelings for his employer, and the safest way of ensuring that the other girl revealed no sign of involvement was for Karen herself to stay aloof from Brad. It wouldn't be easy, but it seemed

46

necessary if the cart was to be kept on the wheels, for the present, at any rate. What was eventually to happen Karen dared not contemplate too deeply. The whole subject was too new and too fraught to be gone into just yet.

The club was on the far side of Colesburg. Driving through the town, Karen gained an impression of wide, oak-shaded streets and gracious residences gathered around the focal point of its one hotel and main shopping area. One or two of the smaller stores were still open, doors ajar to the night, lights spilling welcoming pools over the pavement. Keith pointed out the bank, and the nearest thing to a boutique that the town possessed for Karen's benefit. The hotel lounge, he said, was the regular meeting place for shoppers in need of revival: coffee, in their case.

'Like ladies' day at the races in there from ten-thirty onwards every morning,' put in Brad on a humorous note. 'You'll love it.'

From her seat beside him, Karen could feel the watchful presence of her brother's wife in the back of the car. It made her reticent to say anything which might possibly be misconstrued, so she kept silent, aware of Brad's quizzical glance at her failure to respond to the crack. It was going to be even more difficult than she had imagined to keep up this kind of restraint all evening, she realised. And was she perhaps being a little over-cautious? Denise had taken no pains to conceal her feelings this afternoon when it had been just the two of them, but was she really likely to do the same with the two men present?

It was an unprecedented situation in Karen's experience and there was no one else she could ask for advice. She would just have to play it by ear as much as possible.

For some reason she had anticipated that the club would be a modern building, brightly lit and functional. Approaching the old Colonial-style house via the floodlit drive, she gave a small involuntary exclamation of pleasure, eyes roving the gracefully lofting pillars to the immense upper balcony which ran the whole length of the front, then down again to french windows opened to a wide veranda. Music

47

drifted out to them as they got out of the car, and one or two people called out greetings. The shrubs lining the stretch of lawn gave off an elusive scent in the night air; cicadas chirped shrilly above the occasional hoarse croak of bull-frogs from some nearby waterhole. There was no moon, but the stars were brilliant sparks in a sky velvety soft and black.

Inside there were flowers massed in huge copper urns against white walls, couches and chairs scattered casually about the sanded and polished floor, cream rugs and small blackwood tables to hold glasses from the bar built under the curve of the fine staircase. Brad seated his party close to the latter and ordered drinks, getting to his feet again to say hallo to some people on their way through to the dining room.

'It's very much a community affair,' he remarked to Karen when the two had gone on their way. 'For privacy one must find other places of entertainment.'

'I like people,' she returned without meeting his gaze. 'I like this place too. South Africa is such a mixture of old and new, isn't it? Durban could be a part of the States with that skyline, yet out here it's another world. I'm still not accustomed to all that sense of space.'

'It takes time,' Keith agreed. 'I can't say I'm fully adjusted myself yet. You should go up country, though, for a real idea of what it's all about. In Kruger you're back a hundred years without even trying. Excluding the transport, of course.'

'Plus the refinements offered by the lodges,' Brad added. 'To see the real Kruger you need to rough it with only the bare essentials for survival, though if all you need for satisfaction is a list of animals spotted from a closed car one of the normal organised tours is an ideal way of spending a few days.'

'But you did it the other way,' Karen surmised; and drew a sharp glance.

'Several times. I know a couple of the rangers up there. If you're interested in something a little different from the normal tourist run around, Umfolozi take small parties on what they call Wilderness Trails. No transport except Shanks's pony, and they actually camp out at night. Quite safe. There's a ranger in charge the whole time. Fancy it?'

Denise answered for her, voice a little taut but otherwise quite steady. 'She's hardly going to be here long enough to contemplate that sort of thing, Brad.'

'It only need take a few days,' he returned agreeably. 'As a matter of fact, I was thinking of getting up a small party of my own some time soon. Karen could join us. You too, of course, if you think you'd enjoy it.'

Her laugh was brittle. 'Women are luxury-loving creatures. I'm sure we'd both loathe living rough, even for a few days. Wouldn't we, Karen?'

Caught between two fires, Karen could only murmur noncommittally, 'I suppose so,' and saw Brad's lips take on the familiar slant.

'Shame,' he said. 'But perhaps you're right at that. You both look far more at home in this kind of setting. Two birds of paradise, eh, Keith? You should be proud of having so much beauty in the family.' He drained his glass and set it down with a small thud. 'Everyone ready to eat?'

It was an excellent meal, served with smooth efficiency by two green-jacketed Indian waiters. Brad ordered champagne to go with the oysters, and both red and white wines to suit individual tastes. In addition to the usual courses there was a huge basket of various kinds of fruit to choose from, plus dishes of nuts and olives.

Coffee was thick and creamy and delicious. The men took theirs laced with cognac. By common consent they had retired to the veranda, sitting in cushioned cane chairs around one of the glass-topped tables with the night scents rising in waves from the flower beds below. Karen looked about her at the white-jacketed men and beautifully attired women, at the healthy glow of tanned faces and animated expressions. No boredom here; these people enjoyed being together. A close-knit community, yet one both ready and eager to open its ranks to outsiders.

It wouldn't be hard to be happy in that community, she thought. Not that she had any real intention of staying. She couldn't, could she? There were Aunt Carol and Uncle Tom to consider, for one thing. How would they feel if she wrote saying she had decided not to return home? And there was the problem of Denise. That really made staying on impossible, although neither did she like the idea of leaving Keith alone with a wife who no longer loved him—if she ever had done. She wished she could begin to straighten out her priorities.

It was only to be expected that Brad would ask Denise to dance first, but something inside her tautened unbearably when he did so. They made a striking couple, she had to admit, the golden head poised beside the arrogant dark one.

Keith watched them move indoors too, but there was nothing in his face to reveal what he was thinking. She was perhaps underestimating his powers of perception, Karen reflected. For all she knew he already suspected all she was trying to keep from him. Knowing he wasn't loved by his wife might even be the reason he had wanted her to come out to South Africa in the first place. A sister was some kind of substitute: someone close enough to make him feel not quite so alone.

Only she was letting him down too by refusing to stay. Refusing? Scared to stay would be more like it. She had been here less than a week and already felt the changes taking place inside her. Robbed of the escape hatch represented by her eventual return home she would be left defenceless. And where was the sense in allowing herself to feel anything at all for a man who could have anyone he wanted just by flicking a lean brown finger?

'Did you want to dance?' asked Keith, stirring himself from his semi-reclining position. 'Sorry, I wasn't thinking.'

She smiled. 'That's all right, I'm not all that keen myself just now. What I'd really like is some more of that gorgeous coffee.'

'It's a West African blend,' he said after giving the order to a waiter. 'They always use it here. A bit too rich for some

European tastes.'

Karen laughed. 'It's odd, but I've never thought of myself as a European before. I suppose, basically, it's always been "them" and "us".'

'That's what keeps Britain British,' he quipped. 'Joining the Common Market made no appreciable dent. Let's face it, we're an insular race. Always have been, always will be.'

'Yet you still hang on to your nationality.'

'I'm summing up, not condemning. I'll stay British as long as they'll have me. It's like malaria; once you've had it it doesn't let go.'

'It sounds rather nasty, but I appreciate the sentiment. I hope *you* haven't had malaria, though?'

He shook his head, looked at her a moment and said on a suddenly different note, 'We don't really know very much about one another at all, do we? You were too young to remember Mom and Dad. In a way you were better off. At least you could accept substitutes without too much trouble. I never actively disliked the Bellamys, you know. I just couldn't bring myself to see them in Mom and Dad's place. Perhaps subconsciously I resented them for being alive while our parents were dead.'

'I think they both understood how you felt,' she said softly. 'It hurt them quite a bit, but they did understand. They'd have liked children of their own too, but it didn't work out that way. It's always the ones . . .' She hadn't been thinking about what she was saying, and now she felt herself go hot at the realisation of what she *had* said. Keith was looking straight at her, a wry little smile touching his lips at her abrupt termination. She should have just carried on and finished the sentence regardless, she acknowledged ruefully. Breaking off like that had only served to add point to the slip.

'Don't look so stricken,' he said. 'You couldn't have lived with us for several days without guessing that things aren't all they should be between Denise and me. You might say we neither of us do much to conceal it. Maybe I shouldn't have asked you to come out to us under the circumstances.'

51

'I'm glad you did,' she replied simply, and hesitated. 'Do you want children very badly, Keith?'

He shrugged. 'I did. I can see now that it wouldn't make any difference. Denise and I were washed up ages ago. We should never have married. She needs a man who can give her a lot more than I've managed to provide. Once the initial attraction wore off we began to discover just how little we had in common. It happens in a lot of marriages. Probably because the couple don't stop to think things through before they take the plunge.' He was speaking almost as though to himself, or perhaps as though admitting it to himself for the first time. 'Denise should have married someone like Brad who could have afforded the kind of setting she considers so essential. Being the wife of a plantation manager just isn't *au fait* with her ambitions.' He caught Karen's swift glance and smiled in a way that jerked her heart-strings. 'I'm not a fool. I know darn well she'd ditch me like greased lightning if she thought there was any chance of making it with Brad.'

'You . . . don't think there is?'

'I wouldn't be working for him if I did. They get on pretty well, but that's as far as it goes with him. If he wanted a wife he could take his pick from the Province.' He waited for the waiter to pour the fresh coffee and depart before going on, 'I suppose it doesn't make things any easier all round staying on at Breckonsridge, only I can't bring myself to give it up for the sake of a marriage that's already on the rocks. I love it here and I want to stay.'

There was a lump in Karen's throat which made swallowing difficult. 'You wouldn't care if Denise went, though?'

'Of course I'd care. Divorce is an ugly word in any language. It means failure, and that's something few of us like to admit to. Only neither do I happen to think two people should hang together simply because a bit of paper says so.' He paused, studied her a moment, then said ruefully, 'I shouldn't be doing this to you, Karen. You've your own life to live without sharing somebody else's problems.'

'You're not just somebody else, you're my brother,' she

returned huskily. 'And I'm glad you told me. Really I am, Keith. I'm just sorry it worked out this way. You deserved better.'

'You could say the same for Denise. And I'm not going to deny that having somebody to talk to about it helps a great deal, even if it is pure selfishness on my part.'

Karen lifted her cup but did not drink, holding the delicate china there in front of her with her eyes on the liquid half filling it. 'Do you think Brad guesses how bad things are between you?'

'I've no idea how much he guesses. The only time you know what he's thinking is when he chooses to tell. I don't suppose he'd think it any concern of his.'

'He's your employer. Surely your personal welfare has to concern him to a certain extent.'

'Only inasmuch as it affects my job, and so far I haven't let personal problems encroach on that.'

'So you've never discussed the possibility of you and Denise breaking up?'

'Not at any time. No reason why he should need to know ... yet. What he may have seen for himself is another matter.'

Or what Denise herself might have told him, Karen tagged on mentally, recalling their conversation in the stables earlier that afternoon. Did he really believe that the whole length or breadth of the problem lay only in the direction he had indicated, or had he simply been fobbing her off? Either way, it suggested a closer liaison between the two of them than Keith seemed to realise. His trust in Brad was admirable; Karen could only hope it was not misplaced.

A stiff breeze had sprung from nowhere over the last few minutes, rustling the shrubbery below and bringing a sudden chill to the atmosphere. At Keith's suggestion they gathered their belongings and retired indoors again to the bar, meeting the other two on the way. Without effort the foursome became a sextet, and then grew rapidly into a regular party as small groups merged conversationally.

Denise, Karen noted, talked almost exclusively with Brad,

53

her gestures eloquent, features more animated than they ever were with others. She wondered if anyone else in the gathering was noticing the same difference. For certain, Brad himself was neither blind nor imperceptive; he couldn't fail to be aware of the way Denise responded to to him. So why did he not discourage her? There were ways, surely, of doing so without being too blunt, especially for a man of his undoubted experience. Unless he enjoyed the situation too much to want to give it up. Some men were like that, she believed, always ready to hang another scalp on their belt regardless of who got hurt in the process.

Or he simply might not care either way; even find a mild amusement in the fact that he could so readily draw other men's wives. Whatever the motivation, he was not helping his manager's marital situation in the least.

Karen danced several times over the next hour or so, mostly with the younger male members of the club. Freshening up after a particularly energetic round, she tried to shake off the depression which had claimed her since she and Keith had talked. This holiday had meant so much to her, but it was all turning out wrong. And mostly because of Brad. If he went away again it might help. She resolutely closed her heart and her mind against the desolation that possibility conjured up.

There was a second door to the cloakroom. On impulse she took it, and found herself emerging from the short corridor on to the rear terrace. Round this side of the house the breeze was scarcely noticeable, although the tops of the adjacent trees moved gently against the spangled sky. Immediately below the terrace lay a paved garden area set in the Italian style with stone arches and urns full of trailing plants. A fountain tinkled down from a central display cunningly highlighted by concealed beams in muted colours. Beyond there was a glimpse of the inevitable pool.

The aromatic scent of tobacco drifting out of the shadows at her back gave her warning of some other presence. Brad detached himself from the wall where he had been leaning as she turned her head in his direction, the cigar end glowing in the semi-darkness.

'Like it?' he asked. 'We're rather proud of it ourselves.'

Karen's heart had given one painful thud and then steadied again. When she answered it was with creditable evenness of tone. 'It's certainly different from what I expected.'

'More ... or less?'

She glanced his way briefly, registering the enigmatic expression. 'Both, in a way. Nothing out here seems to conform to any set pattern.'

'You're wrong. We're a very conservative bunch basically. Can't afford to be anything else. Not yet, at any rate.'

He had moved forward until he stood at her side by the low wall, the white dinner jacket stark against the dark mass of vine clinging to the roof support beyond him, fleshless brown hand carrying the cigar once more to his lips. From this angle he seemed to tower over her, vitality in every line of the lean hard body. She felt a peculiar dryness come into her throat, bringing with it a rigidity of limb which would not enable her to move that slight distance away from him that every nerve in her craved for. Something of her emotions must have communicated itself to him, for he glanced down at her with a faint sardonic curl to his lips.

'Relax,' he said. 'I'm not going to bite. Sorry if I ruined your solitude, but I *was* here first.'

'I only came out for a breath of air,' she claimed swiftly. 'It got rather warm in there. I didn't realise you weren't in the bar with the others.'

'Otherwise you wouldn't have risked running into me,' he tagged on for her without inflection. 'Something seems to have been biting you all evening. Care to tell me what?'

No beating around the bush with this man; he came straight to the point. Karen had anticipated no less, but could find no way of answering the query without bringing in matters best left alone.

'Sorry if I've been a bit of a drag,' she said. 'I'm feeling a bit off, that's all.'

'So I gathered. The question is, why?'

'Surely that's obvious. The food, the change of climate...'

'You've been here nearly a week already. If they'd been going to get to you it would have happened earlier. Try again.'

She said stiffly, 'I don't have to try again. My personal feelings are my own concern.'

'Not when they happen to involve me.'

'What makes you so sure they do?'

'Instinct. I seem to have grown two heads again, for some reason.'

'They say two are better than one.' She caught the tightening of his jawline and felt her pulse quicken correspondingly. 'I'm just overtired. It's been a long day.'

'At your age that's a feeble excuse. You found enough energy to dance with everyone who asked you.'

'That was common courtesy.'

'All right.' He dropped the stub of the cigar and trod it firmly beneath his heel. 'So show me the same courtesy.'

She took a breath to steady herself. 'I don't feel like dancing again tonight, thanks. And I think it's time I went back indoors.'

It was a moment before he responded, a dangerous glint in his eyes. 'I think you're probably right. In the circumstances perhaps we'd better call off our ride until you've recovered. It wouldn't do to have you overtaxing your strength.'

She didn't look at him, but her chin jutted a fraction. 'Would you like me to return the car too?'

His teeth came together hard. He made a small movement towards her, then checked. 'I'm not sure what this is all about,' he said, 'but I'll only take so much provocation. If you don't want to use the car then don't, only so far as I'm concerned it's yours while you're here. Right?'

Karen numbly inclined her head. 'If you say so. I'm simply not used to accepting something for nothing.'

He gave a short mirthless laugh. 'If that's all that's worrying you we can settle a price right here and now!'

She was in his arms before she had chance to sidestep

56

his grasp, her head pressed painfully backwards by the pressure of his mouth. The kiss lasted mere seconds, but her lips felt on fire when he let her go. She put up an involuntary hand to them, eyes dark in the whiteness of her face. At that moment she couldn't find one solitary word to say.

Brad's smile held derision. 'Account paid in full. I told you I'd only take so much. Try not to look quite so stricken when you come back indoors or some people might put two and two together. I object to having labels pinned for no adequate reason.'

It was several moments before Karen could summon the will to follow him inside, and when she did it was via the same route she had used to come out. The cloakroom, fortunately, was unoccupied. She took a brief glance in the mirror in passing, surprised to find herself looking no different from usual, apart from the tinge of colour high on her cheekbones. The others were just as she had left them, Brad once more seated beside Denise with attention apparently fully occupied by what she was saying. No one appeared to have connected their absence together as significant of anything but coincidence.

Sliding back into her own seat, Karen forced a smile for the benefit of her nearest neighbour and wished herself a million miles away from this place and everyone in it. There was too much here that hurt.

CHAPTER FOUR

COLESBURG by day proved a town of considerable business activity. The only shopping centre for the whole area, it supplied a variety of goods enough to suit all but the most fussy buyer, if at prices somewhat lacking in the competitiveness which made bargain-hunting worthwhile.

Karen went in on the Wednesday and window shopped along the length of the wide main street, bought herself a caftan in bright primeval colours from the better of the two African handicraft shops, and took morning coffee in the hotel with Molly Gordon whom she had bumped into outside.

Molly was in her late twenties, a cheerful, friendly young woman impossible to feel anything but at ease with. Attractive too, Karen considered, though in a somewhat careless fashion. This morning she wore a denim skirt and a plain white shirt which did nothing for her well rounded figure, the bright brown hair tied back from her face with a piece of frayed ribbon probably borrowed from her daughter.

'I've been meaning to get in touch with you,' she said when they were comfortably seated in a corner of the faintly archaic cane and tapestry lounge. 'I'm having the daughter of some friends of ours in Cape Town up to stay for a couple of weeks, and it occurred to me that she must be about your age. Will you come over and meet her?'

'I'd love to,' Karen responded. 'I'd like to have visited the Cape myself while I'm here, but it's a bit difficult when you've come over especially to stay with people.'

'Yes, I know what you mean. Sense of obligation, and all that.' Molly was smiling as she said it. 'Still, if you did feel you could manage it these friends of ours would be only too pleased to have you stay with them.'

'Oh no, I didn't mean that.' Karen was dismayed that her casual statement should have been taken at its face value. 'I wouldn't dream of landing myself on people without an invitation.'

The other laughed. 'You British! We love having visitors out here, especially from England. There's probably a bit of vanity in it as most of us consider our way of life worth showing off to the less fortunate, but that's beside the point. You let me know when the time comes a bit closer and I'll arrange everything. You really should see the Cape. It's superb. And what about the Drakensberg? Surely Keith is going to get you up there for a few days?'

Karen's answering laugh was wry. 'I can see I ought to have come for six months, not six weeks. Every time I speak to someone they tell me another place I mustn't miss seeing before I go home.'

'That's because we all want you to go back with first-hand experience of every aspect. Some people get off a ship in Durban and take a couple of quick tours up country, then go back thinking they know it all. I'm not saying you'll be like that, only it does seem a pity to waste the opportunity while it exists. Six weeks isn't long, but it could be enough used properly.'

'If one didn't have other commitments. Actually, I've only got about four and a half weeks left now. Time seems to be flying.'

'It always does when you don't want it to. I never know where the days go myself.' Molly paused, considering her with faint but discernible curiosity. 'What do you think of Breckonsridge? Quite a showplace, isn't it?'

Karen said with care, 'I haven't been inside the house yet, but the estate itself is tremendous. Keith did say he'd take me down to the mill some time and let me see the cane being turned into the raw product. I'm looking forward to that.'

'Don't be too eager. Going round those places is like entering the gates of hell; hot and stinking! Not so bad at this

59

time of year, but I don't know how they stand it in mid-summer.' Despite appearances, Molly had not been side-tracked, as proved by her immediate return to the former subject. 'I'd have thought Brad would be laying on some entertainment for you while you're here. The bungalow isn't really big enough.'

'He did arrange the braai for me to meet some people.'

'Oh sure, but that was just a casual affair. I'm talking about the real thing.' Her eyes were sparkling with mischief like any four-year-old. 'Sheer self-interest on my part. Brad hasn't given a good old-style Breckonsridge do for simply ages. He used to put one on each time he came home from a trip and invite everybody. Denise hostessed for him at the last one, as usual, but that was way back in January some time.' She paused a moment, her expression subtly altering. 'Your sister-in-law isn't a very easy person to get to know. To say she's been with us more than a year ... well, I can count on one hand the number of times I've actually spoken with her. Keith usually comes to the club alone, although Denise sometimes makes it when Brad is home.'

Karen met the bland gaze and tried not to let anything show on her own face. 'I suppose some people just aren't natural mixers. I'm sure she doesn't mean to seem stand-offish.'

'Well, she certainly manages to give a good impression of it.' Molly was obviously not the type to withhold an opinion simply because the recipient might have some objection to hearing it. 'Your brother is completely different, thank goodness! He was one of us from the word go.'

'He'll be glad to know you feel that way about him.' Karen sought for some topic which did not touch on Denise in any way and was helped by a sudden quirk of memory. 'Someone mentioned some people called Harlow on Saturday. Haven't they been in America for some time?'

'Five years. They got back yesterday. Haven't seen them myself, but Brenda Girling was over there first thing. To welcome them back, she said. Sheer curiosity would be nearer the mark, I'd say. Not that I can blame her too much. Everyone's been wondering how the twins have turned out. They used to be a pair of young devils by all accounts. Always up to some exploit or other. Still, twenty-five is getting on a bit, and they've been living in a country where sophistication is supposed to be the thing ... or so one gathers from the films. They've probably turned out quite well.'

'You didn't know them before?'

'We only moved up here ourselves three years ago. Before that we were in the Transvaal. Now that's another place ...'

'I ought to see,' Karen finished for her, laughing. 'Next time perhaps.'

'Oh good, if there's going to be a next time that means you like us.' She caught sight of the clock on the far wall and pulled a rueful face. 'I'm going to be late with lunch again, and David said he'd be in at twelve sharp. I hate it when he decides to work close on to the house. He's under my feet more often than not.'

'You have a farm?'

'That's right. Nothing like Breckonsridge, of course. We're mostly fruit with some grazing land thrown in for good measure. We're about thirty kilometres the other side of town, but there's a good road if you do come over. I hear you're using Mark's new toy.'

Karen blinked, then amusedly got her meaning. 'I thought it was a bit underpowered for him, even with a two-litre engine.'

'Oh, lord, do you understand cars? I never could. David says it's like putting a gun in an idiot's hands to let me behind a wheel, but without transport you're sunk in this part of the woods.' She called over the waiter, waving aside Karen's movement to pick up the check. 'This is on me. You can treat me another time. Are you staying in town for lunch?'

'No, I'm expected back.' Denise probably couldn't care less one way or the other, but it was as well to appear to be on normal terms with one's brother's wife. 'I only came in for a look round.'

61

'Saturday is the best time. We have a native market. You can pick up some really good stuff dirt cheap if you don't mind bargaining.'

'I'll try and make it. I'd like to take back some typical African craftwork ... or is that considered too touristy?'

'Depends on the kind of things you choose.' Molly gave her a glance gone suddenly shrewd. 'I've an idea you'll go for the more unusual. You'll have to show me what you buy to take back with you and see if I'm right.'

'I'll try not to disappoint you,' Karen said smilingly.

Outside again in the bright midday heat, Molly indicated a dusty Volkswagen parked towards the front of the tree-shaded forecourt. 'That's me over there. I'll phone you later about Barbara's visit, but do come over in the meantime if you find yourself at a loose end at all. Keith will give you directions.'

Karen took her leave of the other woman and crossed to her own vehicle with the warm feeling that comes from finding new friends. Molly was fun to be with, and from what she remembered of her husband they made a good pair. She looked forward with some anticipation to meeting them both again.

Heading out of the town in the direction of Breckonsridge she reflected that apart from being fun, Molly Gordon was also sharp. If no one else had noted Denise's leaning towards Brad she certainly had. In some ways it would have been a relief to let go and admit that her own feelings for her sister-in-law were less than they should be, but that would have been a betrayal of Keith's trust. Only how much longer could the Grainger household keep up any pretence at all of a normal marriage when people like Molly could so easily see the cracks?

She had gone about three miles and had just passed the crossroads which bordered the outlying cane fields when the engine spluttered and died without any warning whatsoever. She brought the car to a timely stop in the roadside, and sat there for a moment looking wryly out at the sweeping vista of waving cane in which no human figure could be seen. A couple of birds flew high overhead, winging their way south-west towards the bank of cloud slowly piling up on the horizon, but apart from that there was no sign of life anywhere in her immediate vicinity, although very likely there would be cutters at work around the very next bend.

With nothing else for it, she got out and went round to open up the bonnet, peering inside at the beautifully clean engine in the certain knowledge that she would have to have the cause of the trouble staring her in the face before anything could be done. It had been easy enough to bask in Molly's admiration a while ago, but her practical knowledge of the mechanics stopped short at the elementary stage. To her eye everything appeared to be in order. She knew she hadn't run out of petrol because she had filled up only this morning.

The sound of an engine coming along the road from the east jerked her into swift action. She ran back the few yards to the intersection and waved down the fast approaching vehicle with a prayer on her lips that the driver would be of mechanical bent, male *or* female. The strikingly blond good looks and unmasked appraisal of the man who stuck his head out of the wound down window made no immediate impression other than a fleeting reflection that he looked the type who would know something about everything.

'I've had a breakdown,' she said. 'I can't see what's wrong, and wondered if you might take a look for me? I'd be very grateful.'

'Sure.' He drew his own vehicle over and stopped again, then got out and joined her. He was in the mid-twenties, she guessed, and tall enough to top her five feet five by several inches. Something in the greenish eyes made her feel a little uncertain for a moment, then he grinned and the moment was past.

'English,' he said. 'You have to be the one staying at Beckonsridge. I'm Neil Harlow. Not that the name is likely to mean anything to you.'

63

'As a matter of fact, it does.' Karen looked at him with new interest, remembering all she had heard to date regarding the Harlow twins. 'You got back from the States just recently after five years away and you live in a house called Lowlands.'

'That's the name of the estate. The house is called The Folly. Don't ask me why. My father was never a man for revealing past indiscretions.'

Her smile was spontaneous. 'Why take it for granted it referred to his past? Maybe he just didn't like the house.'

He lifted humorous brows. 'Why didn't I think of that? Must be my nature to seek ulterior motives. Let's take a look at this car of yours.'

'It isn't actually mine,' she said, falling into step beside him on the scarred tarmac. 'Brad Ryall lent it to me.'

'Good old Brad.' His tone was light but with an underlying note she found vaguely perplexing. 'He always did have a generous streak. Wrapped up in steel plate, as my sister would say.'

'Serena,' she murmured, refreshing her memory out loud, and he gave her an amused glance.

'Our fame seems to have gone before us. What else have you heard?'

Her eyes sparkled in response. 'Enough to make me wonder if some of your past exploits could stand too close an examination!'

Neil laughed and pulled a face. 'I suppose we were pretty wild. Dad washed his hands of the pair of us at least a dozen times a month.'

'Have you changed?'

His glance passed briefly over coppery hair lifting in the light breeze, lingered a second or two longer on the soft fullness of her mouth. His smile was slow and meaningful. 'I like to think so.'

They had reached the Marina, still standing with bonnet raised. Neil bent to examine the various components, pulled a couple of wires experimentally, then smiled and did

64

something she couldn't see from where she stood.

'Try it now.'

Karen slid behind the wheel and did so, grateful to hear the engine spring to life with a healthy purr. 'That sounds fine,' she said. 'What did you do?'

'Your low tension lead had fallen off the distributor.'

'Oh, I see.' She caught his eye and couldn't keep the laugh from breaking out. 'All right, I admit it. That means as much to me as if you'd said it in Afrikaans!'

He grinned back. 'I've almost forgotten how to speak Afrikaans. Anyway, mechanically-minded women are anathema to the average male. Something to do with undermining one of the last bastions of our superiority, I shouldn't wonder.'

He was leaning on the door as he spoke. Karen saw the smear of grease across one cuff of his immaculate bush shirt and made a small sound of dismay. 'You've dirtied your sleeve. Were you on your way anywhere special?'

'Nowhere where one more black mark is going to make any difference. I understand your brother is Brad Ryall's plantation manager?'

'That's right.' She waited a moment before asking lightly, 'How come you know so much about me?'

'We had a visitor this morning. A Mrs Girling. We neither of us remembered her being a particularly close family friend in the old days, but she seemed to think we should be welcomed back to the fold.' His tone was derisive. 'That woman knows everything happening within a radius of about two hundred kilometres. In the space of an hour we were genned up just about to bursting point with irrelevant detail! Not,' he added smoothly, 'that I consider you a mere detail any longer, Karen Grainger. You've created a definite bright spark in a deadly day. I hope we'll be meeting again soon.'

She smiled at him as he straightened. 'So do I. And thanks again for fixing the car.'

'No bother. Glad to be of service. You shouldn't have any more trouble with it.'

The smile still lingered as she let in the clutch and moved off. She could see him outlined in the mirror, standing with hands thrust into the pockets of his slacks looking after her. When he took one of them out to lift it in a wave she knew he had been aware she would look back.

A self-confident young man, yet with a certain charm about him that lifted him out of the general rut of handsome ne'er-do-wells. She caught herself up there. Wasn't she taking too much as read? For all she knew Neil Harlow had held down a job in the States before returning to his homeland to try his hand at farming. Except that somehow that was not the impression she had gained from what little Brad had said the other day.

Brad. One way or another her thoughts always seemed to return full circle. Since Saturday night she had seen him only once, and that in Denise's company when he had come over to return a book the latter had lent him. He had been pleasant enough on the surface, but impersonal, as though he had lost all interest. She had been relieved when he refused Denise's invitation to lunch on the grounds of a previous appointment. She could not, she felt, have sat there at the same table with the two of them without giving away something of her doubts. She wished she could only be sure one way or the other. Not that it would be easy to accept if her suspicions did turn out to be justified. Keith's disillusionment would probably be the hardest to take. He thought so highly of Brad.

She must stop this speculation, she told herself wryly at that point. Taking things for granted appeared to becoming a habit with her. Innocent until proved guilty beyond all shadow of doubt, wasn't that the British idea of justice? It was one she must start to cultivate a little more herself.

There had been a hope in the back of her mind that Keith would have come home for lunch today, but it turned out to be a forlorn one. She reached the bungalow at a few minutes after one, to be greeted by Denise with icy hostility.

'We don't keep a hotel,' she said before Karen could

offer any explanation of her tardiness. 'Lunch at twelve-thirty may be a bit earlier than you're used to, but it's surely not too much to expect you to make an effort when you said you'd be back. Aaron has been in three times already. Heaven only knows what the curry will be like by now!'

Two spots of colour burned high on Karen's cheeks, but she kept her voice level. 'I'm sorry. I had some trouble with the car.'

'Brad had it checked the day before he let you have it. The mechanic came out specially from Colesburg to collect it while I was there. I don't see how anything could have gone wrong in such a short time.'

'Well, I'm afraid it did.' There was no point in explaining further. 'I'll go and wash my hands while Aaron is dishing up.'

It was a long afternoon, made no easier by the sudden change in wind direction which brought the clouds Karen had seen earlier racing across to cover the whole canopy of sky. For an hour or two they hung there in lowering sullenness before the storm broke with a ferocity that though brief was unvarnished nightmare at its height, each thunderclap loud enough to pierce the eardrums; lightning flashing with an intensity that lit up every nook and cranny in the same electric blue glare. The rain was almost a relief, washing across in a solid sheet to blot out everything beyond the veranda rail for several minutes before dying off to a steady downpour.

Denise had vanished at the onset. Alone in the lounge, Karen curled in a chair with a magazine and tried not to worry too much about Keith out there in the fields. He must have known this was coming; experience would have taught him to read the weather well in advance. He would have taken shelter until the worst was past, was probably at this moment heading home as fast as the car would run through the mire.

When she did hear the car coming along the lane the rain had almost ceased. She got up and went out to the veranda, a smile lighting her features and a jaunty word of greeting on her lips. Both died abruptly as she saw the long low lines of Brad's spectacular estate nose to a stop in the driveway. She stood there in irresolute silence as he slid his muscular length from behind the wheel and came towards her.

'Some squall,' he said, reaching the veranda. There were damp patches on the shoulders of his cotton jacket, beads of moisture glistening in his hair. Eyes assessing, he added, 'Not scared, were you? This was only a mild affair compared with some we get in summer.' The pause was deliberate. 'But that hardly need concern you, need it. You won't be here to see it.'

'It seems not.' Karen pulled herself together, indicating the wet jacket. 'You didn't ought to stand about in that.'

'You're so right.' He slipped it off and slung it carelessly over the back of a chair, ran a hand over his hair. 'I got stuck down on the bottom road and had to dig myself out.'

'No rainproof?'

'We can't all be Boy Scouts.' The mockery was edged. 'That motto might stand *you* in good stead.'

The challenge was an open one, but she had no intention of rising to it. She moved back to the doorway. 'I'll get Aaron to make some coffee. Or would you prefer something stronger?'

'Coffee will be fine,' he said, following her in. His glance went to the magazine lying face down where she had left it, registered the solitary dent in the cushions. 'Denise not at home?'

Karen kept her expression fixed. 'She's in the bedroom. I'll fetch her.'

'No reason to disturb her. She may be asleep.'

'Through that!'

'No,' he said with quiet emphasis. 'After it. Your sister-in-law has a phobia about storms. They exhaust her.'

'Oh?' She was nonplussed. 'I'm afraid I didn't realise.'

'Obviously.' He looked at her and relented a little. 'Denise isn't the type to advertise her weaknesses.'

68

Perhaps it was the way he said it, perhaps merely the words themselves, but something inside Karen sank sharply and sickeningly. She turned away. 'I'll see about the coffee.'

Aaron was through in the kitchen with his wife. Delia spoke only a few words of English, but always seemed to understand what was said to her. She was as fat as a butterball and unfailingly cheerful. Almost before Karen had opened her mouth she had a tray out ready and was bustling about fetching cups.

'Better make it for three,' Karen said, but the African shook his head.

'The missis sleep always after big storm. She not like to be waked. I fetch coffee for two.'

So Brad had not exaggerated. Denise really did suffer a phobia and preferred to do so alone. In which case, how was it Brad knew about it at all? Not the type to advertise her weakness, he had said, yet he apparently was fully cognisant with a very major one—and concerned enough on her behalf to rush here through the storm. Maybe Brad was one person Denise could let herself be weak with; maybe if she herself had not been in the house he would have gone to her, taken her in his arms and held her until the fear was passed. The shaft of pain went deep.

He was standing in the open doorway when she got back to the lounge, smoking a cigarette and looking out at the dripping trees. He turned at her entry, arms bronzed and powerful beneath the rolled sleeves of his shirt. His tie was missing and the top couple of buttons unfastened on a triangle of dark hair. He looked thoroughly at home; casual, yet dangerous too.

'It won't take long,' she said automatically, stopping where she was on the far side of the room. 'Aaron tells me Denise would prefer to be left where she is.'

'He's observant,' came the measured response. 'You should take a leaf out of his book.'

'Or one from yours.' She hadn't meant to say that, it had just slipped out. She bent hastily to plump up the cushions where she had been sitting before his arrival. 'Keith should

69

be here soon.'

'Keith went down to the mill this morning. He won't be back before six.' Brad hadn't moved his position, but his attitude had hardened. 'What was that crack supposed to signify?'

'Does it matter?'

'I think so.'

Her shrug held an assumed nonchalance. 'I was simply acknowledging your perception. My sister-in-law isn't an easy person to know.'

He said softly, 'And you think I know her rather better than I should. Is that it?'

Heart jerking, she faced him squarely. 'Let's just say you've gained her confidence in a way few could.'

'And leave it at that? Not on your life!' He was as cold as steel and twice as inflexible. 'You've had this brewing since Saturday, let's bring it to the boil. You see your brother's marriage apparently coming apart at the seams, you put two and two together and finally come up with another man. As the nearest I'm naturally the likeliest. Is that about right?'

Her throat had gone tight and dry. 'Are you denying it?'

'I don't have to deny it. If I were desperate for an affair I'd hardly choose the wife of the best manager I ever had. That's a consideration you might have taken into account before jumping to conclusions.'

'There's such a thing as one consideration outweighing another.'

'There's such a thing as working out one's priorities, I'll agree. My prime concern is to keep this place running smoothly when I'm not here, and for that I need your brother, not his wife.'

She said huskily, 'That isn't the impression you give. You never left her alone the other night at the club.'

'Correction. *She* never left *me* alone, apart from one short interlude when I slipped outside for a smoke, as you may recall.' His mouth curved sardonically at her slight change of expression. 'In your book it would always have to be the

70

male chasing the female, wouldn't it? Anything else offends your sensibilities.'

'That's not quite true. I realise Denise isn't blameless, but you don't have to go out of your way to encourage her. Without you she and Keith might have made it together.'

'Without me there'd have been someone else. For a woman like Denise there's always a better deal than the one she's got. You should feel sorry for her, not condemn her. Think what it must be like to spend your life reaching for the moon.' He eyed her for a hard moment, then shrugged. 'All right, so I cut out the tea and sympathy altogether, and where does that leave Keith? With no goal to try for here she's going to look elsewhere.'

'And you're afraid he might follow her?'

'There's no might about it, unless he had someone else to care about. He needs emotional commitment the way some men need freedom. He can't exist alone.'

'He did it for years.'

'We all do a lot of things before we find what we're looking for. He found Denise; she found a man able to take her a step up the ladder from where she was. That doesn't mean to say that they were perfectly suited.'

She gazed at him standing there against the doorway, a lean, hardbitten man with a look about him that defied analysis. 'You seem to have made a thorough study of them both,' she said at last on a subdued note.

Cynicism touched his mouth. 'Purely in the interests of the estate.'

'All right, I'll accept that.' She hesitated before going on, 'Supposing I told you you were wrong about Keith?'

'In what way?'

'He knows Denise may leave him and he doesn't intend to follow her. He told me so himself.'

Grey eyes had sharpened. 'If that's so it can only be because he relies on you to take her place.'

'How can I possibly do that? A sister is no substitute for a wife.'

'In the ordinary course of events, no. I just got through

71

telling you how far from ordinary the circumstances are. You'll allow I know them both better than you do?'

'I suppose I must.' Karen could not disguise the bitterness. 'But we're back where we started in that case, because I can't stay on in South Africa indefinitely, whatever happens.'

The arrival of Aaron with the coffee curtailed Brad's reply for the moment. They could only have been talking a short time, Karen realised. It felt more like hours since the car had drawn up outside. Cautiously she probed her own emotions, conscious of relief that her worst suspicions had apparently proved unfounded, yet also of a depression which could only stem from the realisation of Brad's true colours in this affair. Calculating was the best adjective one could in all fairness apply. He needed Keith, and was prepared to go to any lengths to keep him here, including, if necessary, persuading her to remain in South Africa.

And there was the crux of the matter, she acknowledged numbly. It was because of Keith and *only* because of Keith that he had concerned himself with her at all. As a person in her own right she mattered nothing to him in the least.

She poured the coffee in silence when Aaron had departed, taking a seat as far from the one Brad chose as she could get. When she looked up at last he was watching her, expression unreadable.

'Why did you tell me the only thing wrong between Keith and Denise was them not being able to agree over starting a family?' she asked starkly.

'That was a part of it. I saw no reason then to go into further detail.'

'You thought I was too young to understand.'

'I still think you are. Most of it, anyway. You see everything as black or white with no shades of grey. Right now I'm stamped and labelled in that mind of yours as a man without heart for the finer things in life.' The cynicism was back in his smile. 'It's a question of who decides what they are. Do you consider yourself qualified to tell me?'

She kept her tone unemotional. 'I doubt if you'd consider

any woman qualified to tell you *anything*.'

'There you go again!' He looked at his empty cup and put it down on the low table between them. 'Remember what I said about not liking labels pinning on me?'

'I remember.' She refused to let that recollection throw her. 'You also said for no adequate reason. I happen to think I have one.'

'Then we'll have to do something about changing it.'

There was a threat in the way he said it if not in the words themselves. An empty one, Karen told herself. He was simply slipping back into mocking character, the way on might shrug on a jacket. But what she had learned about him this afternoon was not to be lightly dismissed. There was ruthlessness beneath the banter.

'The storm's been over quite a while,' she said as he got to his feet. 'Shouldn't I at least go and tell Denise you're here?'

Brad paused in the act of turning towards the door, looking at her in sudden impatience. 'Don't pretend to be dense. I came at a time when I knew she wouldn't be around because you needed straightening out on a point or two. If the doubts still linger that's too bad, but I don't intend hanging round while you study reactions all over again. Tell her I had an appointment.'

'Do your own lying,' she flashed. 'I'll tell her you've been and she can make what she likes of it. I'm not going to be involved in any of this!'

'You can't avoid it,' he returned hardily. 'You involved yourself by coming out here in the first place. If you want me to stop using Denise as a means of keeping Keith with the estate then you know what to do. Don't get up. I'll see myself out.'

Karen stayed where she was as he went out on to the veranda and swept up the draped jacket. He didn't put it on again but kept it over an arm while he went down to the car. A moment later the engine sprang to life, idled briefly and then took on a deeper note as he engaged the clutch and drove off in the direction of the house.

73

Only then did she move, levering herself slowly from the chair to pile cups and saucers back on to the tray. Brad had been right about one thing, she acknowledged numbly: She was involved. The difference being that it was he himself who formed the main basis of that involvement. And that was something she was going to have to work out of her system before she could bring herself to consider Keith's needs with any real determination.

CHAPTER FIVE

It was half an hour before Denise emerged from the bedroom, and by that time, with the visible signs of Brad's visit cleared away, Karen found it difficult to bring up the matter casually in conversation, such as it was. Her sister-in-law seemed fully herself again, despite the ordeal she must have undergone in sitting out the storm alone. Trying to find a chink in the armour she wore appeared a nigh on impossible task, yet Karen could not bring herself to abandon all hope of reaching her. She was still her brother's wife, and there was some doubt in her mind as to how far his professed indifference to the idea of a separation went.

The storm had been fairly local, it turned out. When Keith got back he reported good weather further down the coast.

'Unusual to get one as bad as that at this time of the year,' he commented over dinner. 'But weather conditions all over the world are cockeyed these days. When we first came out here meteorological reports could predict a change almost down to the minute, but they've been getting further and further off. Can't even blame the Bomb any more, unless it's a delayed reaction.'

'I read somewhere that it's to do with the earth cooling down generally,' put in his wife unexpectedly. 'We're approaching another ice age.' Her smile was wintry. 'Not for another couple of thousand years or so, though.'

'Thank heaven for that! I'd hate to be around when it comes, although I don't suppose this part of the world would be iced over.' Keith sounded forced, as though he had forgotten how to make small talk with his wife. 'There's

75

something to be said for mortality after all.'

They were having coffee in the lounge when the car drew up outside. Karen froze as the visitor came up on the veranda steps, and was conscious of conflicting emotions when Neil Harlow appeared in the doorway.

'Sorry if I've barged in at the wrong time,' he said after she had performed introductions. 'I'd got the impression that everyone ate earlier these days.'

'We do normally,' Denise assured him. 'It's just that Keith was late getting back from Durban tonight. Not that it matters in the least. Perhaps you'd like some coffee yourself ... unless you'd prefer something stronger?'

'I'd happily settle for a whisky,' the newcomer returned easily. 'I came over to see Brad, but he isn't in, so I thought I'd take the opportunity of calling in on Karen.' The dancing gaze turned in her direction again. 'Everything okay with the car?'

'So far.' Karen took care not to look at Denise. 'I'll have to gen up on the mechanics so I shan't have to go stopping other motorists in future.'

'But then you'll be depriving somebody of the pleasure in showing off their expertise. We get little enough opportunity as it is.'

'Do you intend staying on in South Africa indefinitely now that you're back?' asked Keith.

The other shrugged, his expression undergoing an indefinable change. 'Depends on how things go. My sister wants me to stay, but she's in a rather different position. Which reminds me ...' he was addressing Denise again now ... 'we're throwing a bit of a get-together this coming weekend. Renew old acquaintances and make some new ones.' The last a faintly cynical note. 'Can you all make it?'

There was no hesitation in her reply. 'I'm sure we can. Brad said you'd be eager to get back into circulation again. I suppose things have changed a great deal since you were last here.'

'No, I don't think so. Everything seems exactly the same as when we left five years ago.' He didn't say 'and just as dull', but his tone implied it. He weighed his glass a moment, then glanced across at Karen in obvious appeal. 'I thought you might fancy a run into town. We could have a drink at the Albert, maybe even a dance. I'm told they run to a small combo Wednesdays after dinner.'

'Yes, why don't you, Karen?' Denise's tone held just the right amount of sisterly approval. 'You've hardly been anywhere in the evenings since you got here.'

Karen hardly needed any persuasion. The thought of an hour or so of escape from the endless circling of her mind around insoluble problems was a draw in itself. Neil was outside the whole affair, and almost as much a stranger as she was herself. His company would be by way of light relief after the undercurrents she had experienced these last few days.

'I'll need to change,' she said. 'Can you give me ten minutes?'

'I can give you as long as it takes. Serena needs an hour or more just to get ready for bed. Having a sister destroys a lot of illusions!'

'In which case I don't need bother trying to create any,' she retorted on a light note, and went out to the sound of his and Keith's laughter.

In her room she got out the linen skirt and blouse and into a figured blue cotton with short sleeves and scooped neckline. With her face already becomingly tanned she no longer found it necessary to use very much in the way of make-up, and now she contented herself with a fresh rub of lipstick and a brush over her hair.

Neil stood up when she went back, his glance approving her appearance. 'I can see you're a girl of your word,' he commented. 'Exactly ten minutes, no more, no less. You and Serena really must get together. I'm sick of her hogging the bathroom!' His smile at Denise was charming. 'Thanks for the whisky, and the welcome. I'll look forward to seeing you both again on Saturday.'

The night was clear and sweet-scented after the rain, the hills slate-grey shadows against a moonlit sky. The clump of mango trees which marked the entrance to the back lane stood away from the darker mass of the orchards beyond like outriders to a herd of browsing cattle. Then they were running through the cane with the tall fronds swaying to the car's swift passage.

'You seem to be very familiar with the estate,' Karen remarked after a few moments, and Neil smiled.

'I used to know it nearly as well as I knew Lowlands. My father and Brad's were great buddies in the old days.'

She laughed. 'You know, that's the first real Americanism I've heard you use. I'd have thought more would have rubbed off in five years.'

'You could say we were past the impressionable age when we went to the States, if not entirely self-sufficient.' Once again there was that odd inflection. 'Going was one thing, coming back quite another.'

'Then why did you?'

'Needs must.' He paused, changing down for the turn out on to the Colesburg road, blond hair thrown into sharp relief against the darkness of the far window. They were on the straight again before he added, 'Brenda Girling said you'd only been here a couple of weeks yourself.'

'Not quite that yet.'

'Then you don't know Brad Ryall very well?'

'No.' Karen kept her tone carefully expressionless. 'Just as my brother's employer. He was kind enough to loan me the car so that I could get around on my own.'

'Or so that your brother wasn't tempted to sneak off to do the running.'

She looked at him quickly. 'You sound as if you might not like him overmuch yourself.'

It was a moment before he answered, and when he did it was with some bitterness. 'Brad's all right. It's the situation that stinks. At my age I shouldn't have to go cap in hand to ask for what's mine by right.'

'I—I don't understand.' Karen felt thoroughly bewildered. '*Isn't* Lowlands yours and your sister's?'

'Well, yes, only ...' He stopped, gave a wry shrug. 'It's a

long story. Are you sure you want to hear it?'

She hesitated. 'Only if you want to tell it to me.'

'Yes, I do.' He drew the car to a halt under the left side bank of cane, got out cigarettes. 'May as well be comfortable if we're going to talk.'

She bent her head to the flame of his lighter and sat back with a feeling that she was going to regret this later. Yet she could not deny her curiosity either. What jurisdiction could Brad Ryall possibly have over the Harlows' right to run their own property?

'I suppose that not having a mother from twelve on might have had something to do with the way Serena and I behaved during our teens,' Neil said. 'Dad was always tied up with the farm, so we more or less pleased ourselves. Anyway, to cut a long story short, we got in with a bit of a giddy crowd from Durban. They used to come up the coast to one or other of the beach hotels at the weekends and live it up.' He paused, eyes fixed on some point beyond the bonnet of the car. 'A couple of months after Serena and I were eighteen half a dozen of us took another guest's car from the hotel park and drove it hell for leather up the highway till we finally wrapped it round a lamp standard. Nobody got seriously hurt, but the car was a write-off and it cost Dad a packet in fines, plus a ticking off by the court for not keeping us under control. Apparently we were lucky to get off with just that. A couple of the others got a three-month sentence.'

'They'd done something similar before?'

'That and a few other things. So far as Serena and I were concerned we'd learned our lesson, only Dad obviously didn't believe us capable of turning over a new leaf. He said he'd make sure we didn't get the chance to drag the family name down any further. He did too. After he died we found he'd left the whole estate in trust under Brad's administration until we were thirty. We were to draw an allowance from the annual profits but have no say in the running of the place. Can you imagine what it was like hearing that?'

Karen could both imagine and sympathise. To be forced at twenty to submit to the jurisdiction of a man scarcely ten years senior must have had a demoralising effect. She could imagine, too, how Brad would have approached his responsibilities: with firmness, with determination; with vigour, but with precious little compassion.

'Did he suggest you go to the States?' she asked, looking at the cigarette she held in sudden distaste.

'No, that was my idea originally. We have some cousins in Colorado and I needed to get away for a bit. It was only intended to be a for a few months to start with, but it kept on stretching. They ran a dude ranch over there and we got pretty involved. It's a good life if you don't weaken, only I didn't fancy spending another five years on a comparative pittance waiting for Lowlands to become ours in entirety.'

'So you came back to try to persuade Brad to hand over control now.'

'Yes. But for that we needed some kind of lever. That's where Serena comes in. If she marries Brad ... well, it's unlikely he'll keep his own brother-in-law hanging fire for five years.'

A part of Karen's mind didn't seem to be functioning properly; she had heard the words but didn't seem able to assimilate the meaning. 'You mean it was planned even before you set off home?' she got out.

'Oh, not quite as cold-bloodedly as it sounds,' he hastened to assure her. 'He came out to see us when he was over there on business trips, and Serena always was keen. She had a crush on him when she was fifteen.'

'And how does ... he feel about her?'

'Decidedly responsive, judging by the way he reacted to her when he met us in Jo'burg last week,' on a note of satisfaction. 'Not that I blame him. Though I say it myself, my sister is quite a dish!'

Karen didn't doubt it. Neil himself had eye-catching looks, and the two were twins. She barely knew what to say. What *did* one say to something like this when one's own emotions were under stress to start with? It was no use trying to deny that Brad meant anything to her. She had known him less than two weeks yet he already had the power to hurt, even from a distance. From somewhere she found the detachment necessary to carry on.

'I hope it works out the way you want it to. As you said, five years is a long time.'

'Too long.' He leaned an arm along the curve of the wheel to study her, a smile curving his lips. 'You're a great person to talk to, Karen. I've been needing to get that lot off my chest for ages.'

Her answering smile was forced. 'Looking for a reaction, perhaps.'

'You're probably right. There's an element of calculation in all of us when it boils down, but we still have a need for reassurance at times. You didn't condemn either of us out of hand.'

'How could I? I don't know what I might be capable of myself in similar circumstances.' Karen swallowed thickly. 'It can't be easy having your lives run by someone who isn't even family.'

'It isn't. Although I suppose it could have been worse. If Brad's father had been alive he'd have got the job, and believe me, *there* was a hard case! If anything, Brad's been like an elder brother, only it's time he abdicated in my favour.'

'And your sister's share?'

'Well, naturally she'll have that ... if she wants it. As Brad Ryall's wife she certainly won't be in need of money.' He leaned forward and switched on the ignition again with a confident gesture. 'Let's go and dance. I feel in the mood for celebrating.'

Karen wished she felt the same, but her mood of pleasant anticipation had quite flown during the last emotive twenty minutes. What she really wanted to do was to return home to the privacy of her room and try to come to terms with what she had learned. Unfortunately that just wasn't possible. Not unless she wanted Neil to guess the effect his confidences had had upon her. And no one was going to know about that. Not if she could help it. What she felt for Brad Ryall would remain her own personal concern.

Invitations pressed upon her the previous week took up most of Karen's time over the next couple of days, leaving her with little opportunity to brood. Neil had been flatteringly eager to see her again before Saturday, but she had somehow put him off, acknowledging even as she did so that in different circumstances she might very well have found him as desirable a companion as he seemed to find her.

All other considerations aside, there was something basically appealing about Neil Harlow. Mentally, Karen censured the man who had brought the whole situation about. Surely any father who really cared for his children could have found it in himself to forgive them their mistakes before he died.

Saturday brought a recollection of Molly Gordon's reference to the market in town. On sudden impulse, Karen mentioned it over breakfast after Keith had left and suggested that Denise should accompany her.

'I hear it's quite a bargain centre,' she said lightly. 'You could tell me the best kind of things to buy as souvenirs. I'm a complete duffer when it comes to sorting out the wheat from the chaff. Left on my own I'll probably come back loaded down with rubbish.'

'Sorry,' replied the other after a moment during which hazel eyes narrowly examined blue across the table, 'I've got things to do.' She paused then, and seemed almost to relent, features relaxing a fraction. 'The hand-carvings are a good buy, if you can find some individual ones. They tend to follow a few set designs in general. Same goes for woodcuts. In fact, some of those are machined, so watch out. If you like skins make sure they're properly cured. If they're not they'll be stiff and they'll smell.'

It wasn't much but it was something of a breakthrough after the staccato exchanges of the last couple of weeks. Reluctant to let the moment pass, Karen found a scrap of paper and scribbled down one or two notes, looking up with a smile to ask, 'Anything else?'

'Yes, never pay the first price asked; beat them down.' Although not exactly smiling back there was a fraction less coolness in Denise's voice. 'They know a lot of English are reluctant to bargain very hard and they'll try to take advantage if you let them. Will you be coming back for lunch?'

'No, I think I'll stay on in town for a bit, if that's all right?'

'Of course. Why shouldn't it be?' Denise got to her feet, the interlude obviously over. 'You'd better get off right away if you don't want to find everything picked over.'

Karen pushed back her chair and got up, standing there folding the slip of paper between her fingers. 'Are you sure you won't change your mind and come with me?'

'I told you, I've got things to do.' Denise was already on her way from the veranda, tossing a brief 'See you later,' over her shoulder.

Better than nothing, Karen told herself with determined cheerfulness as she went through to her room to collect a handbag. And better by far than the searing attack which had been their only other exchange of appreciable length since her arrival. With some perseverance it might even be possible to get through the barriers Denise had erected against her and convince her that she wanted only to be on friendly terms. What good it would do Keith if she succeeded that far, Karen had not yet fully worked out, but it had to be an improvement on this kind of deadlock.

The Colesburg road was busier than it normally was for the hour of day. Judging from the number of vehicles Karen both passed and was passed by, half the population had elected to spend Saturday morning in town. One ancient tourer held what looked like several families of Africans, all dressed in their best, the children shining like polished ebony. The latter banged on the windows and waved as Karen pulled out to pass them, small faces alight with mischief and the sheer joy of being out and about. Laughing, she waved back before shooting ahead.

The market place needed no finding. All she had to do was to follow the general throng up from the main street to a small area behind the town hall. Stalls were packed together, heaped with produce, with trinkets, with leather and skin work. There were woven baskets, native dolls carved from wood and garbed to represent various aspects of African culture, wooden spears and knobkerries, chairs and stools upholstered in zebra skin, masks with demonic faces; crude but effective.

Some of the stuff was good, a lot more indifferent, with here and there an occasional find of real aesthetic value. One such piece took Karen's eye at once. It was the figure of a heron beautifully carved from a whole buffalo horn so that the tip became the upstretched beak of the bird. Aware of her interest even before she approached closer to the stall, the vendor swept up the bird in one hand and thrust it towards her. 'You like? You take! Ten rand!'

At the present rate of exchange that worked out at around six pounds, Karen calculated. Far too much, of course, and yet how did one begin to price a piece of work which must have taken hours of concentration to complete?

'I'll give you seven,' she compromised hesitantly, and knew she had made a mistake when his eyes gleamed.

'Three,' came a laconic voice over her shoulder, and the gleam changed character as the African began to expostulate vigorously with the newcomer. Karen turned her head to meet familiar grey eyes with fatalistic acceptance.

'It must be worth more than that,' she protested, shelving the question of what he was doing there. 'I really think ...'

'It's worth less than half that in terms of hard cash,' came the unequivocal response. He looked back to the stall holder. 'Three fifty.'

What English the African knew was obviously only enough for the bare necessities of his trade, but it was apparent that he recognised finality in a voice no matter what the language. There was no sign of resentment as he took the money and handed over the bird to Karen. In fact, seeing the satisfied manner in which he folded the notes and tucked them away, she was more than ready to be convinced that Brad had been right. Not that it made any difference to her feelings on the subject. He should have let her make her own mistakes.

'I didn't expect to see you here,' she said as they came away from the stall. 'Markets don't somehow seem your setting.'

'You're probably right.' His tone was casual. 'I saw you trotting in this direction looking all ready to be fleeced when I went along the front in the car, so I came back to save you from yourself.'

'I'm very grateful!'

'Don't take that attitude,' he said with surprising mildness. 'They're naturally out for what they can get, like most of us, but that doesn't mean they appreciate it when they get it. Did you come in alone?'

She looked up at him and away again. 'Denise didn't want to come. She had things to do.'

'I can imagine.' He made no attempt to add to that somewhat cryptic remark. 'I've got a couple of hours to spare. Come and have lunch with me. The Albert puts on a decent meal at weekends.'

Caution fought briefly with temptation and lost. No use telling herself she was being a fool, Karen acknowledged wryly; she already knew it. The only way she was going to be able to put Brad out of her mind was by making certain she had as little as possible to do with him from a personal point of view, yet here she was jumping at the chance to be with him, regardless of what she had learned from Neil.

On the other hand, did what Neil had told her have to be inevitable? Serena hoped to marry Brad, it was true, but how did *he* feel about it? Marriage, he had said a week ago, should be based on compatibility, not emotionalism. He might be attracted to Serena, but it didn't necessarily follow that he would want to cement the relationship. He was more than capable of recognising the motives behind the twins' return home, if it came to that, and he certainly was not the type to be manipulated by anyone. There was comfort of a sort in that latter assessment.

The dining room at the Albert had the same atmosphere of faded gentility as the rest of the place, the flocked green and cream wallpaper, gilt-edged chairs and dark red curtains combining to create a distinctly Victorian air only partially disturbed by the presence of an all-Indian staff. The food was good if unimaginative, the wine South African and delicious.

'Women don't generally have much of a palate for wine,' Brad remarked lightly when she commented on it. 'The subtleties are wasted.'

Karen smiled. 'You're too fond of generalising. Why do men always speak of "women" in inverted commas?'

'For the same reason you just included me in there along with the rest.' His voice held mockery. 'Because it's safer. Start dwelling on individual characteristics and you're getting into deep water.'

There was enough truth in that to make her cautious. 'You think we should all be content to stay in the shallows?'

'Don't put words into my mouth. I said it was safer, not obligatory. The moment we start separating one person out from the rest we're laying ourselves wide open to involvement in their problems on top of our own. It's a personal choice, but one to go into with one's eyes open. Backing out again isn't always so easy.'

'But if the feeling went deep enough one wouldn't want to back out,' she protested. 'Sharing is a part of loving. Not just the good things, but everything, surely.'

'That's an emotional reaction, not a practical one.'

'And you don't believe in allowing emotion to hold any sway.' She said it flatly without expression, aware of his tolerant smile. 'I think you're missing a lot.'

He answered with the familiar taunting inflection. 'You may be right. I'll have to try it some time.' There was a pause and a slight change of tone. 'I understand you've been seeing Neil Harlow.'

'Only once. He brought me down here the other night

when they put on some music for dancing.' She was on the defensive; she knew it, she hoped Brad didn't. 'Everybody seems to be going to the party tonight,' she added quickly.

'So I gather. Curiosity alone would be enough incentive for some. How do you find Neil?'

She was both surprised and disconcerted by the question. 'He seems a very pleasant person,' she said, and saw dark brows lift satirically.

'Is that all? He'll be disappointed. He was a great deal more enthusiastic about you.'

Her reply was guarded. 'That could mean a lot or a little.'

'Which would you want it to mean?'

'I'm not sure. We only just met.'

'And you don't consider it any of my business.' Broad shoulders moved in a shrug. 'Strictly speaking it isn't, but there's nothing in the book against a timely word of warning. Don't start letting your heart rule your head where Neil is concerned. He's the type to take advantage of it.'

'Is this another instance where you're in a better position to know?' she demanded, rattled. 'You take rather a lot on yourself!'

'Don't I? It's as well for you to realise Neil's in no position to support a wife.'

'I do.' Karen hadn't meant to say that, it had just slipped out. She tried hastily to cover up. 'It may come as a shock to you, but I didn't come out here looking for a husband.'

'You may not have thought you did, but marriage is uppermost in the female mind from the day she's old enough to see the advantages in letting a man keep her.'

'That's a cynical attitude.'

'*That* should come as no shock to *you*. You accused me of being one within five minutes of our meeting.' He paused with deliberation. 'How much did Neil tell you?'

It was a waste of time trying to deny any knowledge of what he was talking about. She had given herself away with that too-hasty retort. Fingers curving the stem of her glass, she said, 'Just the bare details.'

'But enough to elicit your sympathies.'

'Up to a point.' She made herself look at him. 'It can't be easy to accept a guardian at twenty-five.'

'It hasn't been easy trying to be one for the last five years,' dryly. 'And guardian is the wrong word. I never at any time had any kind of authority where the twins themselves were concerned. They were too old to be personally responsible to anybody but themselves. The estate is all I control.'

'But that's the whole point, isn't it? Because you have control over the estate you also govern them.' Having brought the matter into the open this far, Karen saw no reason to disguise her views. 'I think their father must have been a very hard man.'

'On the contrary, he was a very concerned one. He wanted to make sure there would still be something left for them by the time they reached an age where they were ready to appreciate it. Given a free rein at twenty they'd have written the whole place off inside of a year. You didn't know them then, you barely know Neil now. In what way does that qualify you to judge the rights and wrongs of the case?'

His tone chilled but did not deter her. 'All right, I'll not argue with that. Only surely the terms were a little too harsh? Is another five years really going to make all that much difference?'

'I hope so.' The brevity in itself was meaningful. He studied her a moment, taking in the soft warm colour under her skin, the determined blue light in her eyes. Almost imperceptibly his expression relaxed. 'You've the makings of a campaigner in you,' he said. 'But you need to select your causes with rather more care. People like Neil are quick to utilise all possible means of support.'

'He could hardly have seen me that way,' she protested. 'I told him I hardly know you.'

'You know me well enough to be driving my car,' with a glint. 'And a pretty emissary is always at an advantage. I would have expected him to see your potential in that direction, though not quite as soon as this. Probably even he expected to have to work on your sympathies a little more before you'd be ready to add weight to his arguments. Still, as we're on the subject I may as well take the opportunity to save him any further effort. Next time he mentions his unfortunate circumstances you'll be able to tell him you did your best but the swine refused to budge!'

'Now you're putting words into *his* mouth,' Karen retorted with some alacrity. 'He never once tried to pull you down personally. As a matter of fact, he said you'd been like an elder brother to him.'

Brad's lips twitched. 'Did he indeed? I can't say I've ever felt in the least bit brotherly towards either of the Harlows.'

He was thinking more of Serena, Karen assumed, watching his slow smile. Partly to break the small silence, but also because she couldn't resist the urge to probe more deeply, she said, 'Doesn't Serena mind waiting another five years to gain her independence?'

'Serena took a degree in independence a long time ago,' he returned levelly. 'In that way she's a far stronger character than her brother. On her own she'd have had a career by now regardless, but she wouldn't leave Neil, so they spent five aimless years playing cowboys. I'd have a great deal more respect for him if he'd found himself a decent job.'

'That would hardly have prepared him for taking over the farm when the time did come.'

'You think he's prepared now?'

'He must be if he's so eager to do it.'

'Eager to sell it, you mean.'

'Mightn't he be that anyway, even if you make them wait?'

'He might. On the other hand, he might just have gained enough sense by then to realise that a home and land have far more value than the amount they can fetch on the open market. That was what his father set his hopes on.'

'He could have made certain by leaving the place permanently in trust.'

'Even assuming I'd have been ready to take it on under those terms, he wasn't the kind to deny his son any chance of ever making good.'

The impatience in his tone was too marked by now to be ignored, yet Karen couldn't stop herself from making one final comment. 'You keep harping on about Neil as if he's the only one to be taken into account. Surely Serena will have some say.'

'Serena is a different proposition. By that time she'll be long married with a home of her own. And we'll leave it there if you don't mind.'

Karen was in full agreement. He had said all that needed to be said. She sat and waited while he settled the bill, got to her feet when he did and passed from the dining room through to the lounge.

Brad lifted a hand in casual greeting to one or two people but made no attempt to approach any of them. From the swift check he made with his watch on sighting the clock, Karen gathered he was rather more pushed for time than he had thought. She was glad of it. Each extra moment she spent with him added weight to the heaviness inside her. But at least she knew now. He was going to marry Serena Harlow. He couldn't have made that clearer. As for Neil— well, he'd be left with egg on his face because it was just as certain that his position would remain the same. None of it bore thinking about.

The Marina was parked some small distance away down the other side of the street. Despite his concern with the time, Brad elected to accompany her to it, taking her elbow to steer her across between traffic flowing quite heavily in both directions.

Karen had the horn bird tucked rather awkwardly under one arm, the base against her ribs, the long slender tip turned downwards. It was instinctive to shoot out a hand to cushion the impact of the small boy who came cannoning into her as he darted from behind a passing car, but impossible to hold on to the bird at the same time. When she picked it up the whole finely tapering beak was splintered and cracked beyond any hope of repair.

Brad drew her to the kerbside before taking it from her

90

to examine it. 'I'm afraid it's had it,' he summed up. 'Someone should teach that little devil to look where he's going!'

The boy had long since disappeared. 'It was an accident,' Karen said dully. 'Just one of those things.'

He was watching her face, his own unrevealing. 'They're individual but not rarities. I'll get you another.'

'I don't want another.'

He frowned. 'You were keen enough on this one when you saw it. Why the sudden switch?'

Impossible to explain why to him when she wasn't even sure herself. Somehow it seemed inevitable that the bird should have been smashed. She shook her head without speaking, saw his mouth tighten.

'I see.' He tossed the bird into a nearby trash can, the movement abrupt. 'That takes care of that.'

The car was only yards away. Brad opened the door for her and put her in, waiting while she switched on. She looked up at him from the open window, lean and hard in the tailored shirt and slacks, face remote like a stranger's.

'I'm sorry if I appeared ungrateful just now,' she began huskily. 'I . . .'

'That's all right.' His tone was clipped. 'You can't help the way you feel. I'm cruel and heartless, and you'd rather die than accept anything from me. The message to Neil remains the same.'

Blue eyes sparked. 'Then pass it on to him yourself. Thanks for the lunch.'

He made no move to stop her as she put the car into motion. When she looked in her mirror he had already vanished among the people still thronging the pavement.

Keith was on the veranda with a drink and a copy of yesterday's local paper when she got back. He thrust the latter aside to greet her, stretching lazily.

'Denise said you'd gone in to the market. Find anything interesting?'

'Just an oddment or two. Nothing much.' Karen took the other chair, dropping her handbag down by the side. 'Is Denise indoors?'

'She's gone over to the house to return a couple of books she borrowed from Brad last week.' He didn't turn his head.

'He won't be there,' she said. To forestall the obvious question she added hastily, 'I saw him in town. He didn't pass me on the road, so he can't have made it back yet.'

'No problem. She'll be able to pop them back in the study herself. The houseboys know her well enough.' The last with a certain dryness. 'How about something long and cool for you? I'll give Aaron a shout.'

'No, I'll do it.'

She got up again and went indoors, took a glass from the cupboard and filled it with freshly made lime juice, then clinked ice into it from the bucket kept constantly replenished. Keith was still sitting as she had left him, but he turned his head at her approach to view her with brotherly tolerance.

'You can't stand it, can you?' he said. 'Being waited on, I mean.'

'Not when I can have the job done while I'm waiting for someone to come and find out what I want,' she agreed mildly. 'You play Lord Jim if you like.'

He laughed. 'It's a way of life that won't be with us much longer. Only the southern provinces still hold on to the old order. Mass unemployment seems to be the desired alternative. At least the domestic situation provides a roof and pay packet.'

'And still would. But through choice, not dogmatism. Anyway, it would do you good to have to fetch and carry for yourself for a bit.'

'Spoken with true sisterly affection!' He sobered suddenly, looking across at her with open appeal. '*Is* it true, Karen? Do you think we've managed to find that affiliation we were looking for?'

'I believe so.' She said it softly. 'There's no reserve left between us. I don't feel there is, at any rate.'

'And you certainly felt it when you first came.' His smile was wryly reminiscent. 'Difficult to credit that you've only been here a couple of weeks.'

Karen found it so herself. She wasn't even the same person. The Karen Grainger of a couple of weeks ago had been a mere girl—not unduly uncertain or lacking in confidence, but unaware. Between then and now stretched a whole gamut of new emotions. If the experience did her no good at present it might prove useful some other time. Some other time? Her throat closed up. Some other time meant some other place, and any place which didn't have Brad in it was totally without appeal.

CHAPTER SIX

THE Harlow homestead lay some twenty kilometres to the west of Colesburg, the house large and well set out and possessing an air of slightly dated respectability which Karen found rather appealing. The resident staff had obviously not neglected their jobs, for the blackwood furnishings gleamed with loving care against freshly painted white walls, while curtains and covers showed every sign of recent attention. All that was needed was the spark of individuality which would bring the place to life again. Karen privately thought that a few strategically placed vases of flowers would have gone a long way towards achieving that effect.

Serena's likeness to her brother was uncanny. There was the same straight nose and wilful mouth, the same thick sweep of blonde hair curling into the nape of her neck. The rest of her was slim and winsomely curved, clad in a brocade skirt and white silk top which made the most of every line.

She greeted all three Graingers with confident appraisal, revealing a flicker of sharper interest when Karen's name was mentioned.

'So you're the one who kept Brad this afternoon,' she remarked on a light note. 'I don't mind admitting I was fuming until he explained the circumstances. It just isn't in him to leave a woman to lunch alone, no matter how hard pressed he might be for time.'

'I don't think he was particularly pressed when we met,' Karen returned, conscious of her brother and his wife listening: 'The service at the Albert is apparently rather slow on a Saturday when the place is full.'

'You mean slower,' put in Neil with a grimace. 'It's not

exactly humming at the best of times. Come and help me play host. You probably know as many people here as I do by now.'

Karen doubted if that were true, but it saved her from facing the question both Keith and Denise would be asking. She should have mentioned her meeting with Brad, she acknowledged. It would have seemed more natural. As it was she had made it look as if she might have had some reason for hiding it. Which she had, of course, but it wasn't one she was prepared to divulge even to her brother.

They were talking with Molly and David Gordon when Brad arrived some twenty minutes later. It helped to have Neil at her elbow as she saw Serena laughingly welcome the newcomer with a familiarity that made her heart ache. Like the rest of the men, he was wearing a lightweight lounge suit, but he still managed to stand out from the crowd.

'They make a good-looking pair,' remarked Molly to Neil in that bland manner of hers. 'Of course, you've known Brad a long time, haven't you?'

'Since we were kids ... though that ten years' difference made a bigger difference then.' His voice had a note of satisfaction. 'Odd how the gap seems to have dwindled.'

'That's because women age twice as fast as men,' Molly laughed. 'Must be all the worry. We spend our best years getting a man, and the rest wondering what on earth we found so marvellous in the thought of being bound hand and foot to a home and family! When I look back on all the things I could have done!'

'Name me just one,' said her husband calmly. 'Your main ambition, as I remember it from school, was always to get married and have at least seven children.'

Neil grinned. 'Did you manage it?'

'No, we stuck at two. But there's time yet.'

'No, there isn't,' retorted his wife with feeling. 'Most times the two we've got seems like seven! By the way, Karen,' she added, 'that young friend of ours is due on Tuesday. I thought you might like to come over on Wednesday.'

'I'll look forward to it,' Karen assured her.

'Nice couple,' murmured Neil when they had moved off. 'A bit staid, maybe, but real nice. Who's this friend you're supposed to be meeting?'

'The daughter of some people they know in Cape Town.'

'A girl! That's different. For a minute back there I was ready to come over all possessive!'

'About what?' she asked lightly. 'We've barely met ourselves.'

'Ah, but the circumstances of our first meeting were exceptional. Did you know that old-time knights were entitled to the hand of any fair damsel they rescued?'

Karen laughed. 'That must have posed problems. What happened if they rescued more than one?'

'Oh, it wasn't compulsory. They simply picked out the best of the bunch, then hung up their swords for all time ... usually on her insistence. No damsel was going to risk the possibility of his fancying some subsequent candidate more than her!'

'What are you two giggling about?' asked Serena, joining them. She was smiling herself, eyes alert and curious. 'Or is it private?'

'Private *and* personal,' her brother returned firmly, and then to the man who had come up behind her, 'Take her away again, will you, Brad. I can't even have a quiet tête-à-tête without being interrogated!'

'It's always good to share a joke,' the older man said on an easy note which didn't quite fit the glance he gave Karen. 'I'd hardly have thought it could be *that* personal on so short an acquaintance.'

'Some friendships get off the ground very quickly.' Neil's hand was on Karen's shoulder, his touch drawing them together. 'We share the same sense of humour, we two, but you and Serena probably wouldn't find it funny.'

'He's more than possibly right,' agreed the latter. 'We never did laugh at the same things. There's a buffet laid on in the dining room, if anyone is interested. No credit to me, by the way. I just left everything to the staff. It was good to come back to the same old familiar faces after all this time. You did a good job keeping them here, Brad.'

'They never showed any signs of wanting to leave. And it's Ron Trent you have to thank for that, not me. He always made sure the whole place was kept the way you'd want to find it if you came back unexpectedly.'

'Good old Ron!' Neil's tone was only mildly satirical. 'Dad must have seen his potential when he first took him on. You haven't met our manager yet, have you, Karen?'

'No,' she said. 'But I'd like to.' She kept her eyes averted from Brad's. 'Perhaps we could find him now?'

'I'll take you across,' offered Serena unexpectedly. 'I believe he's with your brother at the moment. Neil, you might spread the word that the eats are being served.'

Ron Trent was a man in his late thirties, slightly over medium height with a thin, good-humoured face and a hard-muscled frame. He said hallo to Karen pleasantly, congratulated Keith on having such a pretty sister, and looked frankly uncomfortable when his efforts of the past five years were touched upon.

'I had help available when I needed it,' he said with a brief tilt of his head towards Brad, who had accompanied the two girls. 'There's the one you should look to.'

Serena laughed, eyes dancing. 'You'd never find a woman passing up the credit that way. I'm grateful to you both. We both are. It's good to come home and find so little changed.'

'Are you planning to stay for good now you're back?' asked Keith.

'Oh, I'd say so.' Her glance went to Brad, the accompanying little smile suggesting a shared understanding. 'In fact now that I am back I don't know how I ever allowed myself to stay away so long. Not that it will make much difference to Lowlands, of course. Ron will still be running the place for us, won't you, Ron?'

'As long as I'm needed.' Something had closed up in the thin features. 'We'll have to see how things go.'

Meaning that if Serena married Brad there would be nothing to keep him here, Karen assumed with the heightened perception being in love oneself could sometimes bring of emotion in others. Had it happened in the short time since the twins' return, she wondered, or had the feeling lived on through five years of separation? Either way, it placed the man in an unenviable position.

Another couple joined the group, claiming Serena's attention. Somehow Karen found herself standing with Brad on the fringe of the conversation, vitally aware of him, yet unable to think of a single intelligent remark.

'Like another drink?' he asked. 'Or would you rather go and eat?'

'I promised to wait for Neil,' she said awkwardly, and saw his lips thin.

'I'm sure you did. Shattering when it happens like this, isn't it?'

She stiffened. 'I don't know what you're getting at, but ...'

'Oh, come on!' His voice was low but still managed to sear. 'Your face when we interrupted you just now was a dead give-away, even if the way you jumped in on his behalf this afternoon hadn't been. You've gone overboard and you're not sure how to cope with it.'

Right summary; wrong man. Karen gazed at her half empty glass and tried desperately not to let her face reveal what she was feeling at *this* particular moment in time. 'I thought you didn't believe there was any such thing as love at first sight,' she got out.

'I said I didn't believe it had any lasting quality.' Without appearing to move he had eased her away from the others until they stood together within the curve of a window embrasure, his back to the room at large so that her view was limited. Face hard set, he added, 'And what I said earlier still applies. Neil isn't ready to take on a wife. And I don't just mean financially.'

'He's the same age as Serena,' she rejoined softly. 'And you apparently consider her ready for marriage.'

'Age has nothing to do with it. I'm talking about a state of mind. They may be identical in a lot of ways, but when it comes to settling down Serena is way ahead. Neil needs to stabilise, which he won't do whilever there's someone around prepared to encourage him in the opposite direction.'

'Meaning me.'

'At the moment, yes. And it's not just Neil I'm concerned about. He isn't the kind of man you need yourself, if it comes to that.'

She said thickly, 'What *do* you believe in ... computer matching?'

'It might have its points. At the very least there'd be a certain harmony of interests. You have nothing in common with Neil.'

Blue eyes flashed briefly. 'We have one thing,' she said. 'We like one another. I suppose it's quite useless my denying that my feelings go any deeper than that.'

He studied her with a peculiar expression for what seemed like an age. 'Something new has happened to you over the last few days,' he said at last. 'If your feelings for Neil are as superficial as you're trying to make out, then there must be some other cause.'

Karen felt the painful lurch of a heart momentarily arrested. He was too perceptive by half, and frighteningly close to the truth. Whatever else he thought of her, he must not realise that it was he himself who had wrought the changes in her. She could bear anything but that!

'Why don't you just leave us alone?' she said, low-toned. 'We're both old enough to sort out our own lives without help from anyone else!'

'All right.' Eyes cold, mouth taut, he straightened away from her. 'I'll leave you alone. But I may as well warn you that nothing is going to persuade me to hand over control of the estate inside the five years, no matter what happens.'

'I don't care about the estate!'

He looked at her, smiled without humour. 'No, I don't think you do. But Neil cares about it, and the realisation that he isn't going to get it might make for some difference in attitude. Shall you tell him, or would you rather I did it myself?'

Karen felt sick. The whole situation had got out of hand and she could see no way of retrieving it without laying herself open to even greater humiliation.

'It's up to you to do the telling,' she said finally. 'Just leave me out of it.'

'Meaning you're not half as sure of his feelings for you as you are of yours for him?' Brad's tone was sardonic. 'Don't worry, child, I won't give you away. It's one thing to love someone without the feeling being returned, quite another to have them know it. I'll send Neil across.'

Karen watched him move off with an odd sense of detachment. Had he been talking about Serena then? Did he realise the motive behind her interest in him? There had been an edge of bitterness to that latter statement. Perhaps emotionalism had at last caught up with him only to be thrown back in his face. Poetic justice, she supposed one might call it, but she couldn't bring herself to be glad that he, too, was tasting bitter fruit.

The evening passed somehow. Karen was thankful when Keith suggested leaving at ten-thirty. There was a ticklish moment when Neil offered to run her back himself later if she would like to stay on, but the sight of Brad watching them from a distance with the tight little smile still on his lips gave her all the impetus she needed to lightly refuse.

'Tomorrow?' Neil asked on the step as the Grainger family took their leave. 'I thought we might drive down to Durban for the day.'

'Good idea,' Keith put in before Karen could form an answer. 'You only had that brief glimpse when we came through from the airport, and you need a change of scene.'

Karen looked uncertainly towards her sister-in-law who was already seated in the car, but the other's face was averted, her interest apparently gripped by the clipped acacia edging the far side of the gravelled yard. The faint odour of frangipani and wattle wafted in on the breeze, accompanied by the far-off cry of some animal or bird. Only at night was one really conscious of being in Africa at all; like the stirring of some deep down primitive instinct.

'It sounds fun,' she heard herself say without having thought about it. 'What time?'

'Make it nine-thirty, then we can take our time. We'll spend the afternoon in town, then come back along the coast for dinner.'

Used as she was becoming to Denise's lack of small talk, Karen found it an uncomfortably silent journey home. Keith seemed withdrawn too, as though his mind were elsewhere. It was a relief to reach the house, to say their goodnights and go their separate ways. No one suggested touching the flask of coffee left ready for them by the ever-attentive Aaron.

There was no sound from the main bedroom when Karen left the bathroom. She closed her door and took off her cotton housecoat, got into bed and switched off the bedside lamp, then lay there rigidly in the slatted moonlight contemplating the weeks yet to come of the holiday which had already changed her whole life.

She didn't think she was going to be able to take it. Yet what was the alternative? To return home before the stipulated time would be tantamount to throwing her new-found relationship with Keith to the winds. Yet she would be doing that anyway at the end of the six weeks if she refused his plea to stay on.

She couldn't stay on, she thought desperately. Not the way things were. It would be impossible to avoid contact with Brad altogether, and to see him married to Serena would be beyond her. But that was such a selfish attitude, allowing Keith no hold at all on her emotions. Which instinct did she follow?

Her mind was still circling endlessly around the same problems when she heard the other bedroom door stealthily open and close some time later. There came the sound of someone moving along the corridor, a pause, and then the familiar protest of the oldest of the three chairs out on the veranda as a weight was lowered into it.

So Keith couldn't sleep either; had gone out perhaps to

smoke a quiet cigarette and reflect upon his own problems. On impulse, Karen got out of bed and pulled on her wrap again, no set plan in mind other than a need to talk. No lights had been switched on in the house, but the moon was bright enough to illuminate her passage through.

The fair head, just visible over the high back of the rattan chair, didn't move when she went out.

'I heard you come out,' she said softly. 'Are you . . .' Her voice broke off as the head turned a fraction more into the pale light. 'Denise . . . I'm sorry. I thought it was Keith.'

'So I gathered.' The other voice was abrupt. 'He's sleeping the sleep of the just, so I'm afraid you'll have to wait until tomorrow for a shoulder to cry on.'

Karen stood very still, the outer edge of her cotton wrap lifting in the barely discernible breeze. 'What makes you think I need a shoulder to cry on?'

'The fact that Brad is going to marry the Harlow girl. They made their intentions pretty clear tonight. And don't bother telling me it means nothing to you. You've been after Brad since the day you got here.'

'That's not true!'

'No?' Denise twisted in the chair to look at her, eyes shining with some kind of inner turbulence. 'You worked on him to offer you the loan of the car, invited him here when I wasn't around.'

'He came once. And I didn't invite him. I just happened to be here on my own when he arrived.'

'I was in. You could have called me.'

'It was the day of the storm. Aaron said you preferred not to be disturbed.'

'Well, he was wrong. I prefer to be notified whenever I have guests in my home . . . if not at the time, then certainly later.' She paused, her tone taking on a new vehemence. 'You and that brother of yours are about on a par when it comes to self-interest!'

Karen took a long slow breath. 'That brother of mine also happens to be your husband.'

'Try reminding *him* of that. You knew he'd been seeing

Molly Gordon, didn't you?'

'Molly?' Karen's mind went blank. 'You mean he goes over to the Gordon farm?'

'I mean they're having an affair.'

'That's ridiculous!'

'Is it? The person who told me didn't seem to think so.'

Karen said with heat, 'Then the person who told you should get her or his facts straight. Anyone with half an eye could see that Molly is crazy about her own husband.'

'So you only think it unlikely from her side?'

'That wasn't what I meant. I'm perfectly sure Keith doesn't even think of her as anything but a casual friend.'

'Then how come he's been seen over there so frequently? He's never been particularly chummy with David.'

'Perhaps he has but you've simply not been aware of it.' Karen said it carefully, feeling her way. 'And even if he has visited the house once or twice when Molly was there on her own it needn't mean there's anything wrong in it. I daresay it's more than possible that a few might have thought there was something between you and Brad, the amount of time you spend over there.'

The silence seemed to stretch into minutes. Denise sat motionless in the chair, her face oddly luminous in the pale glow from the sky. When she finally spoke it was in tones gone flat and defenceless.

'I suppose I asked for that. But I shan't be going any more.'

'Because he's going to marry Serena Harlow?' Karen still couldn't say it without the accompanying pang.

'That has something to do with it ... though not in quite the way you probably imagine.' Denise paused, spread her hands in a helpless little gesture totally unlike the woman Karen had known this last two weeks. 'You wouldn't understand even if I could find the words to explain. I'm not all that sure I understand myself.'

'I could try.' Karen moved forward a couple of paces to take the chair next to her sister-in-law's, conscious of a curious weakness in her knees. She had no real desire to talk about Brad's relationship with her brother's wife right now, yet this was the closest she was ever likely to come to Denise and she couldn't afford to waste the opportunity. 'Are you in love with him?'

'No.' The single negative somehow rang truer than any amount of more elaborate denials. Mouth wry, she added, 'I'm in love with his life style. It's what I set my sights on as a girl back in Kingston.'

'But you married Keith.'

'Only because his was the best offer I'd had.' Denise glanced Karen's way and lifted her shoulders. 'Sorry if that upsets you, but it was. He was young, go-ahead and ambitious, and he promised me the earth. I believed it because I wanted to believe it.'

'You didn't have any other feeling for him at all?' Karen asked, trying not to condemn her too far.

'I was attracted to him. Enough so as to persuade myself I could settle for whatever he managed to offer. If we hadn't come to Breckonsridge it might have gone on working the way it was, but seeing Brad's place started up all the old obsessions again. Then when he began asking me to hostess for him at various affairs I ... well, I guess I just got into the way of looking on it as almost my own home. He let me choose the colour scheme for the lounge last autumn, and gave me more or less a free hand with the staff when he was away. I suppose if I thought about it at all I saw myself going on being lady of the manor for all time.' She stopped, a small pulse jerking at the base of her throat. 'It was when he came back from his last trip to the States a couple of months ago that things changed. Looking back on it, that must have been when he decided on Serena as his future wife. He stopped giving dinner parties altogether after that. Maybe he reckoned she might not cotton to the idea of another woman having had the run of the house before her. Not that I saw things that way at the time. I thought Keith had put a spoke in the wheel, as a matter of fact. He never actually said so, but he resented my going over there.'

Karen's throat felt tight. She could see the whole thing

now. Brad away so much and happy at first to have some-one conveniently to hand to run his household in his absence, his gradual realisation of Denise's increasing pre-occupation in the place and subsequent steps towards easing her out once he knew he would soon be bringing home the girl he was going to marry. She didn't doubt for a moment that the decision *had* been Brad's, despite what Neil had said of their plans to ensnare him. It was even possible that Serena herself had already known what her future was to be. Just because she and Neil were twins it didn't neces-sarily follow that they shared everything.

'You could hardly blame Keith if he did resent it,' she said. 'He'd naturally want his wife to himself.'

Denise smiled faintly. 'Keith wants the kind of wife I could never be. One who'll give him a couple of kids and be content to stay at home and look after them. I was honest with him from the start about that. I told him I didn't want children cluttering up my life.'

'He may have thought you'd change your mind later on.'

'If he did he was wrong. There are some women who simply don't have any kind of mothering instinct, and I happen to be one of them. My mother was another. Only she didn't know it.'

'What about your father?'

The laugh was short. 'I've no idea. He left three days after I was born and didn't bother to come back. We went to live with my grandparents. They weren't exactly rich themselves, and keeping another two people took just about all they had. I used to creep out at night and go watch the folk in the big houses having a good time, and tell myself that one day I was going to have that kind of life. Only not in that part of the world. I wanted to get right away, start afresh. Keith talked a lot about South Africa when we first met. Land of opportunity, he called it. He'd got enough money put by to make it worth taking a chance on, so I married him. This is where we finished up.'

'It's a very good job,' Karen defended. 'And Keith is happy in it.'

'I know he is, and I'm not saying it isn't. But the comparison is still there. If I'd been free I might have had it all.'

'But if you hadn't married Keith you'd probably never even have come to South Africa.'

'No, that's true enough. In which case I wouldn't have known Breckonsridge existed, and Keith might have found himself a better wife. Someone like Molly Gordon, for instance.'

'Denise, I'm certain there's nothing in that story.' Karen paused a moment, then added with deliberation, 'Although if you really don't care anything for him I don't see why it should bother you anyway.'

'Leave the psychology to the experts,' came the dry retort. 'Happy endings are strictly for the story books. It's a bit late to start rewriting this particular plot.'

'You could at least offer him the option.'

An odd look came over Denise's face. 'You think he'd be interested?'

'I think he deserves the chance to tell you that himself.' Karen hesitated. 'You wouldn't try to persuade him to take you away from Breckonsridge, would you? He's so settled here, and he might never find another position as good.'

'I shan't take him away.' The shutters were back across the hazel eyes. 'I shouldn't have involved you in any of this. You've got your own problems.'

Karen did not refute that. 'I'm glad we did talk,' she said. 'It's helped me to see things a little more clearly.'

'Me too.' Denise pushed herself abruptly upright. 'I'm for bed. That's where you should be too. You could get a chill out here.'

The interlude was obviously over. Wisely Karen made no further comment. She said a brief goodnight and preceded Denise indoors, listening to the quiet click of the other bedroom door with a prayer in her heart for some adequate solution to the mess that was her brother's marriage. Denise mightn't be in love with him, but there had to be some kind of feeling there to have elicited the outburst over Molly Gordon.

God, how foul-minded some people were! It wasn't difficult to see why Keith was drawn to the Gordon household.
They were a family in the real sense of the word; Molly the
kind of woman he had tried so hard to imagine Denise
might one day become. If the latter stayed with him he
would be settling for a lifetime of frustration where his
deeper needs were concerned, yet Karen had a feeling that
he would choose to do that rather than lose her altogether.

And if Denise didn't stay?

She closed her heart and her mind against the alternative.

CHAPTER SEVEN

As in most resorts, the weekend in Durban was a time for family leisure, packing the beaches with bodies and the foreshore with vehicles of all shapes and sizes. All along the seafront work was in progress for the coming summer season, new paint sparkling in the hot sunshine, flower beds refurbished and already bursting into brilliant life. Even the palms seemed freshly got up for the occasion, feathery green heads creating welcome patches of shade along the broad white length of the esplanade.

They had an early lunch at a restaurant overlooking the harbour and yacht basin, spent an entertaining hour or so viewing the teeming sub-tropical marine life of the Oceanarium with its different levels allowing all species to be seen at their natural depths, and emerged from there to an afternoon still young enough for the heat to have in no way diminished.

'We should have brought bathing things,' Neil commented, watching a group of teenagers run shouting and laughing on to the beach from the dormobile where they had changed. 'We could have tidied up in one of the hotels before setting off back.'

'It is really safe bathing?' Karen asked with her eyes on some toddlers down by the water's edge. 'What about sharks?'

'There are nets all along this stretch of coast, and the watch-towers are always manned. There's probably less chance of an accident than on one of your British beaches ... definitely less than on some American ones. Serena and I used to spend hours either on or in the sea as kids.'

Anything rather than learn about farming, Karen surmised and felt the first tinge of sympathy for the man who had loved Lowlands enough to try to preserve it within the family after his death against all the odds. Brad was more than likely right about Neil wanting to sell the place and make use of the proceeds, yet if that were so it was unlikely that another five years would change his attitude. In which case, why not let him do it now and have Lowlands taken over by someone who would appreciate it?

The answer was obvious, of course. Brad had been given a trust, and he would fulfil it to the letter. She felt sorry for Neil, but she could to a certain extent understand that viewpoint.

It was Neil who suggested tea in one of the elegant modern hotels overlooking the beach. Going in through the foyer, Karen was attracted by a display of jewellery in the hotel shop. One type of stone in particular took her eye with its beautifully diversified markings ranging from deepest brown to warm gold; no two alike.

'Tiger's eye,' Neil informed her. 'They're open. Why don't we go in for a closer look?'

At closer range the pieces pleased her even more, especially as the prices were not entirely out of her pocket. Finally she picked out a bracelet and matching ring and said she would keep them on, liking the effect against the cream and tan of her dress. She was disconcerted and not a little perturbed when Neil insisted on paying for them, but her protests went unheeded and she didn't like to make an issue of it in front of the salesgirl.

'It's sweet of you,' she said firmly when they were in the foyer again. 'But you must let me give you the money. I can't accept a present like this from you, Neil.'

'Why on earth not?' He sounded genuinely astonished. 'It's just inexpensive costume jewellery. I wish it were something better.'

'I wouldn't have wanted anything better,' she hastened to assure him. 'I'd be too scared stiff of something happening to it. Only that isn't the point. I'd never have gone in there if I'd thought you were going to do this.'

He shook his head bemusedly. 'I just don't understand what all the fuss is about. Most girls love the occasional present. It doesn't mean a thing. No strings attached. If you make me take the money I'm going to feel a real cheap skate. Is that what you want?'

Karen bit her lip. He had put her in a cleft stick. And perhaps she was taking the whole thing too seriously. 'Of course not,' she said, and made herself smile. 'All right, Neil, I'll say no more except thank you.'

'You're welcome. As I said, I wish it could have been something better.' He looked at her and brightened. 'There's chance yet.'

Not as soon as he might anticipate, she thought wryly. Brad should make it clear to him that he was going to make him wait out the full term as soon as possible. Surely he could have found an opportunity last night if he'd really tried. Anyway, it certainly was not up to her to put the lid on his pipe dreams. Some of the sunlight had gone out of the day. She felt heavy and depressed. It took a real effort to put on a sparkle for Neil's benefit.

They left Durban at seven when the sparkling kaleidoscope of lights was already competing with the stars for brilliance. The foreshore was a fairyland, every hotel front a beacon. In the Amphitheatre gardens tiled pools lay skimmed with gold and silver, while playing fountains reflected a whole spectrum of changing colour.

By contrast, the northbound highway seemed almost one with the dark surrounding countryside until the eyes became accustomed to the change. Occasionally there were glimpses off to the right of small groups of hotels and residences set along the very edge of the shore, then these too became sparser, more isolated, the road cutting in a little from the coast through the vast tracts of cane fields which ran clear up to Zululand beyond the Tugela river.

'We'll have dinner at The Haven,' Neil announced with an air of having just made the decision. 'Then we can cut up through Stanger and round on to the Colesburg road.'

'You haven't forgotten much,' Karen said lightly.

He shrugged. 'Things don't change all that fast in these parts, especially the further up country you get. You're not really seeing as much as you should be seeing. I'd like to take you up to Richard's Bay for the surfing some time. Ever done any?'

She shook her head. 'There are a lot of places I'm not going to have time to see before I go home, I'm afraid.'

'Then don't go. At least, not as soon as you planned.' His glance was swift, expression unusually serious. 'I'd like you to stay on, Karen. Very much. We could have some good times together.' A smile touched his lips. 'We might even find we can't live without each other. Stranger things have happened.'

The words were emotive. So much had happened since Brad had used that very same comment to her the first time she had met him. 'Yes,' she said, 'I'm sure they have. But I don't think I can stay, Neil. I have an aunt and uncle waiting for me to get back.'

'No parents?' He sounded surprised. 'When you spoke about your family before I took it for granted you meant your mother and father.' There was a pause before he added softly, 'That gives us something else in common.'

'Something else?'

'We're both eligible, honey. Life could be a lot of fun.'

'There's more to it than that.'

'Oh, sure there is. But later; after the fun. Burn the candle at both ends while you've still got something left to light it with, that's my recipe for a happy old age. I could live on memories if nothing else.'

She laughed. 'Always providing you survived long enough to do it!'

'All right then, I'll go out in a blaze of high living at fifty. That gives me a clear quarter of a century from now. Long enough for everything I'd want to do.'

But not for her, Karen thought. To love a man; to marry him; to live with him throughout a lifetime; those were the things *she* wanted to do. But not just any man. If she

111

couldn't have Brad then she wanted no one. Not, at least, as she felt right now.

Dinner was all one could hope for in a hotel of the Haven's class. They began with a drink in the bar, then progressed through to the small but well appointed à la carte restaurant to be greeted with cordiality by a youthful head waiter and shown to a table. On Neil's prompting, though with some wariness, Karen chose snails for starters, and was pleasantly surprised to find them delicious, the faint flavour of garlic just enough to titillate the taste buds without overwhelming them. Afterwards they both had langoustines grilled in the shell and served with shrimps and olives on a bed of rice, then finished up with a banana and peach flambé which was prepared at the table side in very spectacular fashion.

'You've spoiled me today,' she sighed contentedly over coffee. 'That was a really gorgeous meal.'

'Glad you enjoyed it.' Neil looked gratified. 'We'll have to do it again.'

'Fine, but I'd be perfectly happy with somewhere a little less exclusive next time.'

His eyebrows lifted in some amusement. 'I've never had any girl look after my pocket the way you do! This place isn't all that expensive.'

'I'm sorry.' She was uncomfortably aware of having presumed too much. 'I thought as you were still living on an allowance from the estate . . .' She let the sentence trail off.

'Oh, it isn't so small that I can't afford to bring you out for a meal. Some people might even consider it generous.' His shrug was light. 'It's all relative, isn't it? Compared with what's tied up in the estate itself, Serena and I are living on peanuts.'

'But Lowlands brings in a constant income. How long would the capital last if you lived it up the way you were talking about in the car?'

'Long enough. Besides, there are one or two deals I wouldn't mind getting into, given the wherewithal. If you think small you stay small. I intend to be big ... one way or another.'

'What if Brad fails to do as you want?' she ventured, not quite meeting his eyes.

He laughed. 'With luck, brad is going to be far too busy adjusting to married life to be bothered with Lowlands. That sister of mine takes some living with.'

Karen could imagine. So would Brad, if it came to that. They made a good pair, she had to admit, but would it really be a compatible one? From what she knew of Serena Harlow the two of them were in some ways too much alike: strong-willed, independent, and capable of ruthlessness when it came to getting what they wanted. Could two such people ever hope to achieve a balance? It was difficult to believe that Brad didn't know exactly what he was doing, but love was supposedly blind. The odd thing was that she herself could see him so clearly; acknowledge his arrogance, his cynicism, even his occasional flashes of cruelty, yet still love him as she did. Perhaps that was what real love was all about: the ability to comprehend, and make allowances.

It was going on for ten when they were ready to leave. There had been several other cars parked close to the Volvo when they had come in, but now it stood isolated from the next group. Karen could see something odd about the set of the vehicle as they were walking towards it, but it took Neil's sudden furious exclamation to pinpoint the cause. Each of the four tyres had been slashed beyond hope of repair with some sharp instrument and were flat to the ground. They stood together staring at the damage, Karen shocked and distressed, Neil swearing under his breath.

'Who would do something like this?' she said at last. 'It's sheer vandalism!'

'That's right. We have it here too.' He started to say something else, then glanced at her and checked himself. 'Maybe I shouldn't complain. It isn't so long ago since I was engaged in more or less the same pursuits.'

'There has to be a difference,' she returned in quick instinctive defence. 'Yours was a spur-of-the-moment jape;

this was calculated.'

'Not necessarily. Not that it matters either way. It certainly can't be driven. I'll phone through to Serena. If she's out Ron will have to come and get us.'

'Supposing neither of them is available?'

'Don't let's cross any more bridges until we come to them. Come inside with me. There might still be some funny guys hanging around.'

The management was profuse in its expressions of regret over the incident, but predictably disclaimed all responsibility. They were, however, offered free usage of the telephone in reception, the manager himself making the connection for them.

Neil didn't say a great deal. He simply explained the situation and asked Serena to bring the station waggon out to pick them up.

'She'll be here in about thirty-five minutes,' he said when he had replaced the receiver. 'We can have a drink while we wait.'

'The bar is about to close, sir,' put in the hovering manager. 'But you are very welcome to take a drink in the residents' lounge. I'll have a waiter come to you.'

The residents' lounge was sparsely populated, the arrival of strangers at such an hour a matter for obvious conjecture. They took seats close by the door and ordered drinks from the Indian waiter who materialised wearily at Neil's elbow.

'It's very quiet here,' Karen commented after he had fetched their order and departed again. 'Too far from Durban for the crowds, I suppose.'

'Too early in the season. They'll be fully booked in December and onwards.' Neil grimaced into his glass. 'There's more ice than liquid in here. Must be trying to get rid of it. Sorry it had to turn out like this.'

'It's hardly your fault. Anyway, it's been a lovely day, and I've seen Durban. Nothing can spoil that for me.'

'You've only seen a fraction of it. There's the Beria yet, and the view from the Bluff. Then it's only a short drive

114

out to the Valley of a Thousand Hills and the Nagle dam. Now *that* you should certainly see!'

Karen was laughing and shaking her head. 'You sound just like Molly Gordon and all the others. Semi-Americanised you may be, but you're still a South African at heart ... and proud of it too.'

His mouth widened in response a little sheepishly. 'You're right at that. Only don't tell Serena. She'd laugh her head off at the idea of me being patriotic.'

So Serena could be insensitive too, even where her brother was concerned. Strange, Karen reflected, how one took it for granted that twins were always attuned emotionally. Or it could be that only applied to identical twins, of the same sex, the same cell. It was a thought-provoking subject, though not one she wished to study at too close quarters in this particular case. In fact the less she considered Serena Harlow at all the better it would be.

Conversation had lapsed somewhat before the allotted time was up. Brad might have had a point there, she reluctantly acknowledged. She and Neil did not have a lot in common. It was with some small relief that she heard the latter, who was facing the door, announce his sister's arrival, then she saw his expression change and twisted her own head to see Brad following the other girl into the lounge.

'We took a look at the car on the way in,' he announced shortly. 'I'll get the garage in Colesburg to send a pick-up out for it first thing tomorrow.' He eyed the barely touched glass in front of Karen with a certain grim disfavour, passed a brief glance over her and looked back at Neil. 'If you're ready we'll get straight back. I'll drop you two off and then take Karen on.'

'You said you'd be on your own,' Neil said *sotto voce* to Serena as the older man preceded them all towards the door, and received a bland gaze in return.

'You mean you assumed I'd be on my own. You didn't give me a chance to tell you Brad was there when you phoned. Naturally, he wasn't going to let me drive out here on my own at this hour. You know Brad. What difference

115

does it make?'

'None, I suppose. Except that I'd have preferred to be taking Karen home myself.'

'Well, I'd say you've had it, chum.' Her smile at Karen was without malice. 'Saved by the bell. I hope you're not going to rail against fate as well.'

'It seems we all have to accept the inevitable,' she returned with amazing steadiness, and drew a laugh.

'Keep thinking that way, honey. It might save a lot of time. Come on, both of you, or that mood Brad's been in all the way here is going to erupt into something I'd rather miss out on.'

Karen could guess at the cause of that mood. To be interrupted in the middle of a quiet evening with the woman he was going to marry and dragged all the way out here constituted a more than adequate reason for annoyance. Yet what else was Neil supposed to have done? It would have taken ages to fetch a taxi from Stanger, even if someone had been willing to come.

Brad was already at the rear door of the estate when they got outside. He opened it without speaking for Karen to get in, then said something to Serena who promptly slid in beside her, leaving Neil no alternative but to take the front passenger seat. They set off almost before he had settled himself, turning out of the hotel drive and on to the main road with the atmosphere inside the vehicle vibrating with unspoken thoughts.

Karen recalled little of the drive to Lowlands, although Serena kept a conversation of sorts going throughout the journey. Brad drew up in the forecourt but kept the engine running while the two Harlows got out of the car.

'You'd better come in front,' he advised Karen. He waited for her to comply, then lifted a hand in brief farewell to the two outlined on the porch before moving into gear and away down the drive.

'Had a good time?' he asked brusquely when they were on the road again and heading for Colesburg. 'You certainly made a day of it.'

'That was the idea.' She heard the faint note of defiance in her tone and carefully ironed it out. 'It was an unfortunate end to an enjoyable trip. Will Neil be able to claim on his insurance?'

'Providing he's covered against this kind of thing. I wouldn't worry about it. He certainly won't.'

'You're wrong, you know.' It was neither the time nor the place, but she couldn't let that statement pass. 'He was very upset by the whole business.'

'I'm sure he was. He'd have been anticipating a nice long drive home with a chance to park along the way. You underestimate your own appeal.'

'That's more than can be said for your opinion of your own powers of assessment!' She was tense and quivering, every word a sharp little spike in her chest. 'You're determined to see no good in him!'

'That's not true. I'm merely determined that *you* see him realistically.'

'I already do.' They were cutting through the suburbs of the town now, passing houses still ablaze with lights. At one, set slightly above the level of the road, a party seemed to be in progress. Karen could see right into the wide lounge through french windows thrown open to the night, where men and women stood around in groups with drinks in hand, or danced to the strains of some music unheard above the noise of the engine. Fleetingly she wished she were a part of that lighthearted set; wished she were anywhere but here with Brad in the car like this. She could be honest and tell him she had no emotional interest in Neil, but that was too much like baring her soul. Having him think her besotted with the younger man at least provided a defence of sorts.

Something slithered from her lap to the floor of the car with a tinkling sound. When she touched her wrist she discovered her bracelet was missing. She put down a hand and felt around until her fingers encountered the smooth stones, picking it up with the intention of sliding the bracelet into her handbag until she had an opportunity to examine it more closely.

'Broken?' Brad asked with a sideways glance.

She shook her head. 'It doesn't seem to be. I don't think the clasp can be very secure. I ought to have checked it before we left the shop.'

She had spoken without thinking. Feeling the sudden stiffening in his attitude, she wished she had held her tongue. But it was too late for that.

'You let Neil buy it for you?' he asked on an ominous note.

'I ... well, yes, I suppose so.' She hastened to add, 'He insisted on paying for it. I didn't want him to.'

'Then you shouldn't have allowed it.'

She said defensively, 'It wasn't expensive, and I did ...'

'I'm well aware it wasn't expensive.' The interruption was terse. 'It's tourist stuff, mass-produced and practically worthless in terms of value.'

'To you perhaps. I happen to like it.' She was sitting stiffly upright, mouth held firm by sheer effort of will. 'And value is based on more than just cost. That's a snob assessment. If everyone used money as their only yardstick the world would be in an even sorrier state than it is already!'

'That wasn't what I meant, and you know it.' Brad's voice was clipped and dangerous. 'Personal presents from a man to a woman are open to misconstruction at the best. *Cheap* personal presents become an insult!'

'That's not fair!'

'Of course you wouldn't think so. Or wouldn't admit to thinking so. It came from Neil, therefore it's to be treasured regardless.' He paused, drew in a long slow breath as if to stop himself adding something to that statement. 'Someone needs to straighten him out on a few matters.'

'You're not to interfere!' The words were jerked from her. Hands clasped tightly in her lap, she gazed out to where the headlights cut a powerful swathe through the darkness ahead, illuminating the cane lining the roadside. 'It doesn't have anything to do with you,' she tagged on with rather more control. 'You told me yourself only yesterday that you were in no way responsible for his personal behaviour. I won't have you speak to him about me.'

'*You* won't have it?' He said it so softly it was barely audible, but there was no mistaking the sudden contraction of muscle along his jawline. 'Perhaps you could do with a little straightening out yourself.'

'Why? Because I refuse to acknowledge your right to do and say exactly as you please?' she demanded thickly. 'Well, I'm sorry, but I don't happen to think you're the kingpin a lot of others make you out to be. What I think *or* feel about Neil is entirely my own affair. Just stay out of it, please.'

Brad made no answer. Mouth clamped, hands taut on the wheel, he sent the big car forward in a powerful surge that pinned her back in her seat and created minor havoc among the swiftly flowing banks of cane. They finished the journey in a silence broken only by the roar of the engine. Karen could feel her heart thudding against the wall of her chest with sickening intensity, but she was otherwise numbed through.

When they finally drew to a halt outside the bungalow she reached blindly for the door handle without looking at him. There was a moment when she thought he was going to say something; a moment when she would have welcomed almost anything rather than this simmering animosity. Then she was standing on the tarmac and the car was pulling away again, the tail lights dwindling until they vanished around the near bend in the narrow lane. She had never felt so alone in her life.

Barbara Bray proved one of those restlessly energetic people many find somewhat exhausting after a relatively short period. Karen found her a tonic: an out-and-out extrovert with a bubbling sense of fun which invited one to forget the trials and tribulations of living and simply enjoy it to the hilt. She was extremely attractive in a gamin kind of way, her dark hair cut very short and swept carelessly across her forehead above an impishly tilted nose and sparkling brown eyes. Only an inch or so taller than Karen, she still somehow managed to make the latter feel almost petite.

'I'm just starting to accept femininity,' she confided with a grin that first afternoon. 'I always had a hankering to be a boy. On my twenty-first in a few weeks' time, I'm going to stun everybody by turning overnight into a raving beauty with flowing tresses and plunging necklines. I'll have to wear a wig for a bit till my own grows, but the effect should be quite good, don't you think?'

'Devastating,' Karen agreed, and they both laughed, the weighing up completed. 'How about bringing the date forward and trying your new look out at the club on Saturday? Neil Harlow suggested making up a foursome ... if you don't mind a blind date?'

'He's the one who just got back from the States, isn't he?' Barbara looked interested. 'I'd love to go to America, wouldn't you?'

'I never really thought about it. Coming out here was the journey of a lifetime to me.'

'Yes, you must find it very different. I'd like to visit England some time, too.'

'Well, if you do I'm sure my aunt and uncle would be only too glad to have you stay with us for a while,' Karen said. 'I shall be going home myself in another couple of weeks or so.' There was bleakness in the thought, but it was time she began accustoming herself to it.

'Now why is that acceptable but my suggestion that you should go and stay with Barbara's family not?' asked Molly in mock indignation from the other side of the sunny farmhouse kitchen where she was busy preparing tea. 'I can't for the life of me see any difference!'

'The difference is that I hadn't met Barbara when you did suggest it, so the whole family would have been strangers.'

'Does that mean you'd be willing to come to Cape Town now that we have met?' put in the other girl on a pleasantly eager note. 'We'd love to have you. Tell you what, why don't you come on down with me when I go back and spend your final week with us? We could have a great time!'

'That's not a bad idea.' Molly looked suddenly doubtful. 'Or do you think Keith might be hurt if you left early? He was only saying the other afternoon how fast the weeks were going.'

Had there been any lingering doubt in Karen's mind regarding the relationship between her brother and this woman, the casual reference to his visits would have been more than enough to dispel them. Fleetingly she wondered if Keith ever spoke about his marital troubles to Molly, but somehow she doubted it. He would come here to forget about it for a while if anything. Thinking about the way things had been in the Grainger household this last few days brought a hollowness inside. Since their talk the other night, Denise had barely strung two consecutive words together, and her quota of cigarettes had practically trebled. Last night there had been a flaming exchange between her and Keith, the rise and fall of their voices audible to Karen as she lay in bed if not, blessedly, the words themselves. They couldn't go on much longer the way they were. Something had to give soon.

'I'd have to ask him what he thought,' she prevaricated. 'I must say I'd like to see the Cape.'

It was left like that for the time being. Studying her brother covertly that evening after dinner, Karen knew she would be leaving it altogether. He looked drawn and weary, with apparently not even the spirit left to make an effort, for he had hardly spoken a word since coming in.

Denise had retired early on the pretext of a headache, leaving the two of them alone together. It would do him good to talk it out, Karen felt, but short of pitching right in on the subject herself there seemed no way of getting him to open up. He just sat there half hidden behind the newspaper, although she was almost certain he wasn't reading it. He was too still, for one thing; none of the little rustles normally associated with the close perusal of a page of newsprint. It was there as a front, an excuse not to have to find something to say.

She got up and wandered restlessly across to the door, standing with her back against the jamb looking out at the moonless night. The faint aromatic odour from the eucalyptus trees across the lane touched her nostrils. That was a scent she would always in future associate with Africa, she thought, regardless of origin. Odd how great a part the sense of smell played in fixing memories, so that one whiff of it even years later could bring back a whole scene in intimate detail. Perhaps it was fortunate that the cigars Brad smoked were of such a rare brand. That was one memory she could do without reminding of—providing she ever did manage to forget.

'How did you get on with Molly's visitor?' asked Keith unexpectedly, and she turned back into the room to find him looking at her over the top of the lowered newspaper.

'Oh, fine,' she said. 'Barbara's a real live wire. We're meeting her in the morning for coffee, then Neil is going to take us both up to Kranskop and over on the Tugela ferry to visit Ntuli's Kraal. He's a sculptor, isn't he?'

'One of the best.' He folded the paper with meticulous precision and laid it down beside him on the couch, squaring it with the cushion before carrying on, 'Neil Harlow seems to have taken quite a shine to you. Not that I blame him,' looking up with a quick smile. 'I just wondered how you felt about him, that's all.'

She said carefully, 'I like him a lot, but that's as far as it goes. I doubt if it goes any deeper with Neil either. We're just friends.'

He nodded. 'That's what I thought myself, only Brad appears to have a different impression.'

Her lips tightened abruptly. 'It doesn't have anything to do with Brad.'

'Ordinarily it wouldn't. I suppose his connection with the Harlows makes a difference.'

'He told you about that?'

'No, Molly Gordon did. I gathered it was fairly common knowledge.'

'I don't think it's supposed to be. Neil would be devastated if he thought everyone knew his circumstances.'

'He obviously didn't mind you knowing.'

'That's the whole point. He told *me* himself. Brad surely should have kept his own counsel on a matter like this!'

'I'm quite sure he has. Unfortunately things like this have a way of getting around a fairly close-knit community. I daresay it was common knowledge even before the twins left for the States.' Keith paused and eyed her for a moment. 'You're very quick to jump to Neil's defence.'

'Isn't that what friends are for?'

'And Brad? You don't count him as a friend?'

Something closed up in her throat. 'Brad doesn't need defending. He's more than capable of looking after his own interests. I don't like what he's doing to Neil making him wait out the full ten years before he hands over the estate. It smacks almost of despotism. It isn't even as if it's going to make any difference in the long run.'

'There's every possibility that he doesn't have any choice in the matter. For all you know it could be legally impossible for him to alter the terms of the trust, especially in the knowledge that Neil would immediately up and sell the place out of hand.'

'That's not the impression he gave me.'

'Then you've discussed it with him?' The blue eyes had sharpened. 'Did Neil put you up to it, Karen? Did he try to use you as a lever?'

'No, he didn't. It simply came up in conversation, and I saw no reason why I shouldn't state my opinions, that's all.' She came away from the door, desperate to change the subject. 'Shall I make us both a drink?'

'Nothing for me, thanks, I'm not in a drinking mood.'

She wasn't herself, but she went across anyway and poured a generous measure of lime, splashing in a minute quantity of gin and adding ice.

'You'd never make a barmaid,' Keith observed as she turned round with the glass in her hand. 'The ice is supposed to go in first.'

'I know. I always forget.' She looked at him irrresolutely, trying to summon the nerve to ask the questions she so badly needed answering. There seemed no way of doing it with tact, yet she couldn't just stand around waiting for him to make the first move towards discussing things. He had said once before how much it helped to be able to talk to her, so why not now? Or was she being too presumptive; sticking her nose in where it wasn't wanted? There was only one way to find out.

'Keith,' she said. 'What about you and Denise? I may be speaking out of turn, but it worries me to see you this way.'

His expression softened. 'Thanks. It means a lot to me to know you care. I honestly can't tell you what's going to happen because I'm not all that sure myself. She's been so jumpy lately.' He hesitated before going on slowly, 'You know, in all the time we've been married we'd never had a real stand-up blazing row about anything up until now. She always refused to fight. Said it was degrading.'

Karen could imagine; she could even understand. One only retaliated when one was deeply hurt, and to be hurt that way by a man it was necessary to have some depth of feeling for him. Hope stirred faintly within her. Last night Denise had apparently forgotten her self-imposed restraints sufficiently to lash out at Keith. Didn't that then indicate that *some* kind of feeling existed in her towards her husband? One emotion could beget another, it was said, therefore it might conceivably follow that jealousy could arouse a dormant love—and Denise certainly had not been left unmoved by the suggestion of Keith's involvement with Molly Gordon.

'Perhaps,' she said, 'it might be a good thing that you've begun to let things out instead of bottling them up. It's like taking the lid off a pressure gauge.'

Keith's smile was faint but warm. 'Sometimes I think you're a whole lot older than your birth certificate says. One of these days you're going to make some man a rare wife.'

Not unless she could learn to feel for someone else the

way she felt about Brad, Karen reflected hollowly, and she couldn't bring herself to believe that possible. She wasn't even sure that love itself was a worthwhile emotion when it brought so much unhappiness in its wake.

CHAPTER EIGHT

KEITH had already left the house when Karen went out for breakfast. Denise was still seated at the table, the inevitable cigarette between her fingers. In the sharp morning light it was all too easy to spot the tell-tale lines of strain about her eyes and mouth. She looked older than her twenty-eight years right now.

'Going out?' she asked, noting Karen's immaculately pressed linen safari suit. 'Don't forget your gun!'

Karen laughed, not resenting the satire. 'We're going sightseeing.'

'We?'

'Barbara and Neil and myself.' The pause was brief enough to be almost non-existent. 'Why don't you get ready and come with us? I'm sure Keith wouldn't mind lunching on his own for once.'

'Keith won't be back till late. He's driving out to look over some land Brad is thinking of buying up country.' It was said without expression. 'I'll stick around here, thanks. It's too hot to drive anywhere today.'

They would hardly be in the car all day, Karen reflected, but she knew that wasn't the real reason for the refusal. Denise simply didn't want to be with anyone. It was a re-action she could understand but not condone. Wallowing in one's unhappiness alone was no solution to anything, and got dangerously close to self-pity. Life had to go on even if it wasn't possible to have exactly what one wanted from it. That was one conclusion she had reached during the previous long night.

'If you're thinking of bringing Neil back to dinner would you tell Aaron,' Denise said before getting up from the

126

table. 'He likes to have his numbers straight.'

'I don't think it's likely. He's picking Barbara up this morning and bringing her into town, so I said I'd take the car in and leave it there for the day to make things easier.' Karen glanced at her watch. 'I'm not going till tennish. I wish you'd change your mind and come with us.'

'No, thanks. I have things to do.'

She conceded defeat. 'Perhaps another time, then.'

'Yes, that's right.' There was an odd little smile on Denise's lips. 'Another time. Enjoy yourselves.'

That smile lingered in Karen's memory for some reason during the drive into town. She had a feeling, growing slowly into a conviction, that some decision had been reached with regard to her sister-in-law's future plans. Whatever they were, one could only trust they did not spell finish to her marriage. Surely somehow a total break could be avoided.

Neil and Barbara were already waiting for her in the hotel lobby, so deep in conversation that it was a moment before they realised she had arrived.

'Neil was telling me about his cousin's ranch,' Barbara said with enthusiasm as Karen took her seat. 'It sounds tremendously adventurous!'

'But darned hard work too,' he put in quickly. 'Bob doesn't carry any passengers, staff *or* family. Only the paying customers enjoy the full benefit.'

'But you must have liked it,' she insisted, 'to stay out there so long.'

Neil caught Karen's eye and shrugged. 'It was as good a place as any to hang out. Anyway, Serena was keen.'

Until Brad had offered a more attractive alternative. Karen resolutely turned her thoughts from that direction. Today she was going to forget all about Brad, forget about everything but enjoying the moment.

She looked away from the other couple for a moment towards the outer doors at present opening to admit more people, and felt her heart give its customary jolt as her eyes found the tall familiar figure in slacks and casual jacket in

127

the midst of them. There was no getting away from Brad at all. He was everywhere.

He appeared to be with two other men at present, all three deep in some discussion which carried them past her own party to a corner some yards away. Brad took a seat at right angles to hers but directly in her line of vision. The quick turn of his head to summon a waiter caught her unawares. She saw his eyes flick from her face to those of her companions, the faint lift of a brow as he took in the closeness of the other two chairs and the sudden twist to his lips as his gaze came back to her. Karen nodded back coolly, then made herself concentrate on what Neil and Barbara were saying, stretching her mouth into a smile when they did in appreciation of a joke she had heard only as a meaningless jumble of words.

'Shouldn't we be getting started?' she asked when another few minutes had passed with neither of the others showing any sign of wanting to make a move. 'If we're going to get back at a reasonable hour we ought to be on our way.'

'I suppose you're right.' Neil stretched easily from his semi-leaning position. 'Come along, then, girls. Regard me as at your service for the rest of the day.'

From the corner of her eye, Karen saw Brad say something to his companions and then get to his feet. Her whole body felt stiff and immovable as he came over to their table.

'I didn't see you when we came in,' he said pleasantly. 'Going on somewhere?'

'Kranskop and across on the ferry,' Neil answered. 'I don't think you've met Barbara yet, have you? She's staying with the Gordons. Barbara, this is Brad Ryall.'

Brad came further into Karen's vision as he leaned over to extend a hand. His manner was easy. 'Molly mentioned you were due round about now. I hope you enjoy your stay.'

Barbara sparkled at him unselfconsciously. 'I'm sure I shall. Aren't you the one Karen's brother works for?'

'That's right. Come over to Breckonsridge if you're

interested in sugar planting at all, and I'll show you round. In fact,' he added, 'we may as well make a party of it while we're about it. Say lunch on Saturday?'

'A braai?' Karen asked, and felt his gaze drop towards her.

'You'd rather a more formal affair?'

'Oh no! No, of course not.' She was swift to deny the implication. 'I think the South African idea of weekend lunch ideal. It's a pity our own climate isn't more reliable. I'm sure a lot of people back home would love to be able to plan a meal outdoors without having to think of what the weather might be like several days ahead.' She was talking too much and too fast, the words themselves inconsequential. 'I shall miss that kind of thing,' she finished lamely, and drew a sardonic smile.

'I'd try to make your impression of us sound rather more solid if anyone asks. We tend to be a fairly touchy race.'

'But forgiving with it,' Barbara put in laughingly. 'Anyway, Karen likes us. She said so.'

'She did? You must have struck a sympathetic chord.' Subtly his tone altered. 'If Keith is in when you get back this afternoon will you tell him I'll be over about six.'

So Denise was not even to be indulged with a phone call. Karen nodded without looking at him, heard him proffer a general farewell and was sliding back her chair even as he moved away, anxious to be clear of the place before he found any reason to return.

'Can we go now?'

'Eager beaver,' Neil said with affection, slipping a hand through an arm of each girl as they came away from the table. 'And I always thought the British took their sight-seeing so steadily!'

Karen knew Brad watched them depart, and the knowledge contributed nothing to her spirits. The day had gone flat, like a wine left to breathe too long. If she could have thought up some plausible excuse for despatching the other two without her she would have used it without hesitation. She and Denise made a fine pair, she reflected numbly. It was only to be hoped that the latter would make a better adjustment than she herself was doing so far.

Long before they eventually returned to town in the late afternoon it had become obvious that the inclination of their little trio had subtly altered during the course of the day. Not that she minded. Barbara and Neil suited one another admirably; different in many ways yet somehow achieving a balance. At one point when the two girls had been left temporarily on their own, Barbara had asked in forthright fashion if there was any understanding between Karen and Neil, her relief unconcealed when Karen had assured her there was not.

'He's so different from the boys I get to know back home,' she confided. 'So sure of himself, for one thing. I do like people who know where they're going.'

Always providing they were going in the right direction, Karen thought dryly, but refrained from saying so. Who was to say which was the right direction for Neil? Brad didn't necessarily have the answer. What was good for one might not be good for another. Neil needed to be free to follow his own ambitions, not tied to a home for which he had no feeling.

It was with little regret that she opted out of the latter's suggestion that the three of them picked up a fourth and extend the day into dinner and dancing at one of the coastal hotels, pleading tiredness after the day's activities.

'Why don't you and Barbara go on your own?' she suggested as though the idea had just that minute occurred to her. 'You can run her back to the farm first to change, then carry on to Lowlands.'

They took little persuading. Barbara gave her a wide warm smile from the window of Neil's car. 'See you Saturday, if not before.'

Saturday at Breckonsridge: laughter and sun-kissed lawns; the smell of charcoal and sizzling steaks. It was where she had come in, so surely an appropriate place at which to go out. Karen supposed Serena would be there to play hostess this time. She was suddenly glad she had never been invited to see the interior of the house. Somehow it made it easier to accept the image of Serena as mistress there.

Darkness fell before she reached the turn-off for the lane leading in through the rear of the estate. Taking the first bend, she saw the headlights of another vehicle angling in behind her from the opposite direction. The toot of a horn as the car caught her up told her who it was even before her eyes had registered the shape of the bodywork behind the lights. She hooted back, lifting a hand in quick greeting to her brother's dimly seen shape behind the wheel. She had imagined Keith would be home by now. It was almost seven o'clock. Brad had said about six, so he must have been expecting him earlier too. No doubt he would have been and gone by now. She certainly hoped so.

The sight of the all too familiar estate car parked alongside the short drive despatched that hope in short order. Karen pulled in behind it and got out, waiting for Keith to join her before making any attempt to enter the house.

'Heavy day?' she asked as he came up rubbing his left shoulder in an easing motion, and he grimaced.

'A long one anyway. Enjoy yourselves?'

'Very much.' She indicated the other car. 'We saw Brad in town this morning. He said to tell you he'd be over about six.'

'Then he's had a long wait,' ruefully. 'I'd have been back ages ago, but I had a tyre blow out on me and found I'd forgotten to put the jack in the boot. I flagged down four cars before I found one that fitted.' He paused at the head of the steps as his employer appeared in the lounge doorway. 'Sorry you've had to hang about, Brad. It's been one of those days.'

'It isn't important.' The other man sounded abrupt, his features austere in the glow from the outside lamp. 'You'd better come on in. There's something you have to know.'

Karen felt her whole body tense involuntarily in sudden awareness of what he was going to say. 'It's Denise, isn't it?' she got out. 'She's gone!'

Grey eyes narrowed to her face. 'You knew she was planning it?'

'No.' Karen met her brother's stunned gaze with compassion. 'But I should have known she was going to do something. She acted so oddly this morning.'

'How do you know she's gone?' Keith's voice was low, his face stiff with the effort of control. 'Did you see her?'

Brad shook his head. 'Aaron says she left before lunch. She left you a letter. It's on the table.'

He shook his head again as Karen moved to follow her brother indoors, standing aside to let Keith pass, then coming further out on to the veranda himself to join her.

'Let him read it alone.'

She gazed back at him numbly for a long moment, then turned to lean against the rail and look out over the darkened garden, her throat aching. It took no great feat of imagination to know what Keith was going through in there right now. The expression in his eyes had been that of a man suddenly and shatteringly aware of having lost. If only she had stopped to think this morning she might have realised what Denise was planning and been able to stop it—or at least persuade her to postpone her departure until Keith himself had a chance to speak to her. Now it was too late.

'You may not have known she was going to do this today,' Brad said quietly behind her, 'but I'd be willing to bet you know more about it than Keith obviously did. Supposing you come clean.'

She didn't look round. 'Does it really concern you all that much?' she asked on a cool hard note.

'It concerns me.' The compression of his jaw was there in his voice. 'There has to be some reason why Denise should decide to do this now. Some new reason. I think you know what it is.'

Fingers curved tightly over the smooth wood, she said, 'If I do it will be Keith I tell. She's *his* wife.'

'Is she?' Keith was standing where Brad had stood moments before, the single sheet of notepaper crumpled in his hand. Facing him, Karen felt her heart go out to the defeat in his eyes. She made a small movement to go to him, then checked, conscious of Brad's looming presence at her elbow.

'*Do* you know what made her decide to take this step, Karen?' Keith asked into the pause, and her pulses jerked.

'I have an idea what might have contributed, but I'm not prepared to go into it out here.'

'She means she's not prepared to tell you anything while I'm here.' Brad moved sharply. 'I'll sit in the car while you two talk.'

'No, stay.' The younger man's tone was stronger, the request almost a command. 'Karen, it isn't going to make any difference Brad knowing one more or less detail about Denise and me. I'm sure he's guessed the situation before this.'

'All right.' It would perhaps have been more fitting to suggest that return indoors before blurting out what she had to say, but there was something about being out here in the night air that helped a little. Finding the right words was the greatest problem. Finally she knew there was only one way to say it, and that was straight out. 'Denise believed you were having an affair with Molly Gordon.'

The silence seemed to grow in direct proportion to the seconds ticking by, the night sounds separated from the three of them standing there on the veranda like a picture gone slightly out of focus. Keith was the first to speak, his face reflecting his emotions more plainly than any words.

'That's ridiculous! Molly wouldn't contemplate an affair with anybody, much less me. We're not even attracted to one another, except as friends. How on earth could she have suspected anything else?'

'Wives ... and husbands too, if it comes to that ... are apt to regard any kind of association with members of the opposite sex with suspicion,' Brad said. 'You've been visiting Sunnyside fairly frequently these last few weeks. It was odds on somebody was going to put a name to what you and Molly were up to when David wasn't around.'

'We talked, that's all. She's a comfortable person to be with.'

'You don't have to justify yourself, Keith,' Karen put in swiftly. 'I told Denise it wasn't true.'

'Obviously she didn't believe you.' Brad glanced from her to her brother. 'So what are you going to do about it?'

The shrug deceived no one. 'What can I do? She says in her letter she was taking a plane out this afternoon but doesn't say to where.'

'The airport authorities will be able to help you there. You can go after her; bring her back.'

'Supposing she won't come?'

'For God's sake, man!' The impatience was scarcely held in check. 'If she hadn't wanted you to look for her she wouldn't have left the note in the first place. Telling you she was taking a plane was as good as announcing her destination. If you want her back you go and fetch her. It's as simple as that.'

Keith's smile was faint and wry. 'I only wish I had your confidence.'

'Call it a calculated gamble. Just get your skates on and start moving.'

Keith half turned back into the room, then paused. 'What about things here? I can't just walk out on the job.'

'I'm telling you to do just that,' Brad said evenly. 'Let me worry about things here. And you needn't concern yourself over your sister either. She'll be taken care of.' The glance he sent her way challenged her to question that statement. 'I already told Aaron to cancel dinner. Karen will come back to the house with me.'

The other man was looking at him oddly. 'You were that sure I'd want to follow her?'

'Like I said, I'm a gambler.' Briefly his glance found Karen's again. 'Nothing was ever gained by dithering.'

'Point taken. I'll get those skates on.'

'I'll pack you a few things,' Karen offered. 'You'll need to get your passport, won't you, just in case?'

'How about cash?' Brad asked, and was moving even as

he spoke. 'I'll have some ready for you over at the house. You can drop Karen off at the same time.'

Things moved swiftly after that. Seated at her brother's side in the car, Karen wondered how long it would be before she saw him again. If Denise had left the country it could take days to trace her through to her eventual destination, always providing she had left a trail to follow. Karen herself was not yet convinced on that point.

'Take care of yourself,' she murmured when they reached the house, and he gave her a strained smile.

'Sorry about all this, Karen. It's been a lousy holiday for you so far.'

'No, it hasn't. And you'll soon be back. *Both* of you.' She leaned across and put her lips to his cheek as Brad came across the courtyard towards them, then got out of the car.

'That should see you through a few days,' said the latter, handing over a thickly wadded envelope. 'Cable if you need more. And call through from the airport, will you, once you know something.'

Karen stood with him watching the tail-lights vanish through the gates. Brad was the first to move. 'Let's go inside. I think we could both do with a drink.'

One of the houseboys was crossing the big open hallway, white jacket immaculate. He gave Karen a grin of recognition before vanishing through a door opposite the one Brad made for. From inside the lounge looked even bigger than ever, but warm and inviting at the same time. Karen sat on an oatmeal lined sofa in front of a niche displaying several porcelain figures which even her relatively uneducated eye could tell were collector's items, and admired a giltwood bergère upholstered in green velvet. Against the opposite wall stood a marble-topped console bearing a basketful of coral and dried seaweed, sponges and shells, the overall effect strangely beautiful. The carpet beneath her feet was soft gold and thickly piled.

She took the glass Brad handed to her with a murmured word of thanks, conscious of her dependence on him with Keith gone.

'Do you really believe Denise intended him to go after her?' she asked unsteadily.

'I think she left the option open. Tracing her movements would have been a great deal more difficult without that letter.'

She could only hope he was right. Keith might have managed to convince himself that he could cope with the break-up of his marriage until tonight, but he must realise now how far he had been deceiving himself. If Brad were wrong and Denise did intend this break to be final she hated to think what it was going to do to her brother. Yet, equally, should they come together again it would surely have to be on different terms from those of the past?

'Stop dwelling on it.' Brad was watching her face. 'They have to do their own sorting out. Nobody else can help them there.'

Her eyes were dark. 'They might stand more chance of making it work if they got away from Breckonsridge altogether.'

'They might. On the other hand, there's more to a fresh start than a change of environment.'

'Meaning you don't want to lose Keith.'

'No,' he said roughly, 'I don't. Neither will he want to go. And if Denise has any feeling for him at all she won't make him choose.'

'But she may find it difficult to come back here under the circumstances. The comparisons still exist.'

'That's where her adjustment has to start.' He was leaning forward with his elbows resting on his knees, revolving his glass slowly between his cupped hands. 'I didn't say it would be easy.'

'And Keith's?' she said softly, already knowing the answer.

'His has already begun. He'll settle for a childless marriage providing he's met halfway.'

She swallowed on dryness. 'A compromise? Nobody wins; nobody loses. It seems ... incomplete.'

'It's better than nothing.'

The tone of his voice drew her eyes to him. 'You don't really believe that,' she said flatly. 'I think *you* would rather finish up with nothing than accept less than the best.'

Some slight change of expression passed fleetingly across the strong features. 'You could be right.' He came abruptly to his feet as one of the servants appeared in the doorway. 'Come and eat. Keith won't reach the airport before nine.'

The anticipated call came through at nine-thirty. Brad took it in the study, coming back to the lounge bare moments later to nod his head reassuringly in answer to Karen's unspoken question.

'She apparently boarded a flight to Mauritius at four o'clock. There's a night flight leaving in fifteen minutes. He's going on it. I told him to stay there a few days till things are straightened out.'

A few days. Karen thought of the lonely bungalow and wondered how she would get through them. Time went so slowly when one was waiting for something to happen. And it would bring her dangerously close to the end of her holiday, unless she arranged to stay on longer. But that was no answer either. If and when Keith did bring Denise home they were going to need time alone. Her presence would only be an added complication.

'Not afraid of staying in the bungalow alone, are you?' Brad asked, reading at least a part of her thoughts. 'Aaron and Delia are only across the back.' The pause was marked. 'I'd ask you to stay here except that the arrangement might cause some local comment. There's nothing narrower than the community mind.'

It wouldn't exactly delight Serena either, Karen conjectured. She summoned a smile. 'I'll be fine, thanks. How long do you think it will take him to find her once he reaches the island?'

'Depends how quickly she wants to be found. A few hours maybe. I doubt if he'll bother to contact us until he knows for sure what's going to happen.' He took in the dispirited droop of her slim shoulders and softened a little. 'You need a good night's sleep. Come on, I'll take you round. Tomorrow things won't seem half as bad.'

The veranda and lounge lights were still on, although Aaron had apparently retired to his own quarters for the night. Brad accompanied her inside, declining her offer of a drink with a decisive shake of his head.

'You'll be better off getting straight to bed. I'll come round again in the morning. We might use the opportunity to take that ride at last. Rennie could use some real exercise.'

Her head lifted. 'Won't you be too busy for that?'

'I doubt it. Keith has things pretty well in hand, and the overseer knows what he's about. Enough so as to be capable of carrying on for a few days. All I need to do is check with him morning and evening. The rest of the time we'll spend together.'

With or without Serena? Karen wondered fleetingly, but something within her shrank from asking the obvious question. Let Brad sort it out as he saw fit.

'Tomorrow,' he repeated. 'Tennish?'

'Fine.' Her throat hurt. 'And thank you ... for everything. You don't know what it means to have someone there to rely on.'

His smile was brittle. 'A pity it couldn't have been Neil. Lock up as soon as I leave.'

He was gone before she could reply, dropping down the steps to stride off into the darkness without a backward glance.

CHAPTER NINE

THE chestnut mare proved as easily controllable as Brad had promised, much to Karen's secret relief. That first morning they rode out around the perimeter of the estate and across a stretch of the veld, taking it slowly so as to allow her muscles time to adjust.

There was a particular delight in the feel of silken movement beneath her, in the tang of hide and leather mingling in her nostrils, the warmth of the sun on her arms below the short-sleeved white shirt; even more in the sight of Brad's strong hard back and dark head ahead of her when he urged Caliph into the lead where the terrain roughened. He sat a horse in the manner of one born to it, his control of the mettlesome Arab unobtrusive yet never in doubt. To achieve that kind of rapport one needed to ride like this every day, Karen acknowledged, and refused to allow the depression to swamp her anew. Time enough to live with that later. For now she would take things as they came and try not to think of the future.

Despite what had been said the previous night, she had not expected to spend another evening at Breckonsridge, and was both surprised and disconcerted to find that Brad had apparently taken it for granted.

'Perhaps you'd prefer to go out somewhere?' he queried, sensing her reaction. They were seated on the veranda at the bungalow after a late lunch, Brad with lazily stretched legs and a cigarette smouldering in his fingers. He hadn't altered his position, but there was something in his voice which drew her eyes swiftly to him.

Did that mean he would rather go out himself? she wondered. And what about Serena? She wished she could pluck up the nerve to ask that very question, yet at the same time had no real desire to know the answer. He had promised Keith he would look after her, and he apparently was taking the promise seriously. It might even be that Serena had objected to the inclusion of a third person in their plans over the coming few days, preferring to keep her own company rather than share Brad's attention, except that such petty behaviour was not at all in accord with Karen's impression of the other girl, brief though their meetings had been so far.

'I don't mind,' she said at last, receiving no help from her scrutiny of his impassive features. 'Whatever *you* want to do.'

His smile was tinged with mockery. 'We'll compromise and drive down to the coast for dinner. I'm not in the mood for the club tonight.'

She hesitated before saying, 'You don't have to go out of your way to entertain me, you know, Brad. There must be other things you'd rather be doing.'

The mockery deepened perceptibly. 'There are other things we'd both probably be doing. What are you hoping for? That Neil will come looking for you? I wouldn't count on it.'

'I don't.' She could think of nothing to add to that bare denial.

'Good.' It was obvious he did not believe her. He came to his feet, slinging the stubbed end of the cigarette out over the rail with more than a hint of intolerance in the line of his mouth. 'I'll pick you up at seven-thirty.'

Karen didn't wait to see him drive off. It was too hot out here. Hot and sultry. She hoped they were not in for another storm. Aaron was refilling the ice bucket in the lounge. She told him she would not be needing a meal that evening and suggested that he and Delia took the rest of the day to themselves.

The house seemed unnaturally quiet after they had left it. She rested a while on her bed but could not induce sleep, her mind flitting from one thing to another without coherence. Eventually, because she could stave it off no longer, she let herself think about Brad, wanting him there with a hunger that hurt more than anything she had known before. Only he wasn't for her. He belonged to Serena. All she had was the loan of him for a day or two. And it was going to hurt even more when those days were over.

The afternoon brooded to a close at last, though darkness brought little respite from the closeness of the atmosphere. Karen was ready at twenty past seven in a long jersey silk skirt and shirt blouse almost the same colour as her hair. Her heart beat a rapid tattoo against her ribs when Brad came up the steps promptly on the half hour.

'The resilience of youth,' he commented dryly, viewing her from the doorway. 'We're in for a storm later, but we should beat it back. Want to risk it?'

She said, 'Do you?' and saw his lips firm.

'If you're going to hand back every query that way I'll save you the trouble by not asking anything else. Bring a wrap. It may be hot now, but it will cool off when it rains.'

'Perhaps we should go to the club after all,' she said impulsively. 'At least it's closer.'

In the slight pause something sparked suddenly and decisively in the grey eyes. 'If that's what you want. I'll phone through and make sure of a table.'

She was aware of the difference in his mood all the way out to Colesburg and wished she had had the sense to keep her mouth shut. Their arrival together without Keith and Denise would be sure to cause comment, and the last thing she wanted was for anyone to know where her brother and his wife were—particularly why. Brad would have thought of that this morning; it was hardly his fault that she herself had proved so dense.

The moment she heard the music coming from the dining room she knew there had been more than one reason for his reluctance to come here tonight. It was obviously one of those special occasions he had spoken of, the place thronged with people in party mood and dress. Had it not been for her he would no doubt have been bringing Serena. She stole a glance at him as he took her wrap from her, but he was giving nothing away. They were here, and he would make the best of it.

As she had anticipated, there was curiosity over the absence of Keith and Denise, but Brad passed it off easily by saying he had sent Keith on a job for a few days and Denise had elected to go with him. If anyone thought it odd that both Graingers should be away when they had a guest in their home they kept it strictly to themselves, although Karen sensed speculation in the glances which followed her and Brad to their table.

'You should have told me,' she murmured unhappily when they were seated. 'I thought there would only be a few people here tonight.'

His shrug was not designed to reassure. 'It had to come out sooner or later. This way might be the best after all.'

Karen's brow wrinkled a little. 'I'm not sure I understand. Are we talking about Keith and Denise?'

'No,' he said with deliberation, 'we're not.' His gaze went to the floor where several couples gyrated slowly to the rhythm of the excellent quartet. '*There* is what we're talking about.'

Barbara and Neil looked totally engrossed in one another, her hands on his shoulders, his curved close about her back, their faces almost touching. There was an aura about them of the kind which drew indulgent glances, an unmistakable oneness that brought a swift ache to Karen's throat. Whatever had happened, it had happened to both of them with equal intensity and speed. She was glad for them, but she envied them too. How wonderful to be so totally oblivious to everything but each other in that way. It took everything she had to bring her eyes back to Brad without revealing her deeper emotions.

'They go well together,' she said. 'You knew they'd be here?'

He nodded. 'Serena mentioned it this morning when she rang.' The pause was brief. 'She also said Neil plans to go back to Cape Town with Barbara to meet her parents.'

142

Karen said brightly, 'The Harlow family move quickly, don't they? Neil might even beat her to the altar yet!' She bit her lip, seeing his expression tauten. 'I'm sorry, I shouldn't have said that. I'm glad they both feel the same way.'

'It does help.' He was still watching her, his mouth cynical. 'Sometimes a kick in the teeth is almost a kindness. If you've any sense you'll start putting him out of your mind from now on.'

'If love had anything to do with sense we'd none of us have much to worry about,' she flashed back without pause for reflection. 'You may not think so yourself, but it isn't something you can turn off and on like a tap! All right, you've shown me what you set out to show me. Now can we please leave it alone!' Her voice had risen slightly towards the last; she caught the eye of the woman at the next table and felt the warmth creep under her skin. She didn't need to look at Brad to assess his reaction.

'We'll leave it alone,' he said, 'when you show signs of pulling yourself together. You're not in love with Neil; you're in love with your own image of him.'

She swallowed thickly. 'And Barbara, I suppose, sees him as he really is.'

'I've no idea. I don't even know the girl. Neither am I particularly interested. It's you I'm concerned about.'

'I'm flattered.'

He drew in a quick harsh breath. 'Don't talk to me that way. You've lost him; accept it.'

'I never had him.' She could have added she had never wanted him, but there seemed no point. 'And stop treating me like a child, Brad. I'm more than old enough to be both seen *and* heard!'

'It's the implications that needle. You can be as sarcastic as you like about my motives, but don't expect me to just sit here and take it on the chin without retaliation.' His voice was clipped. 'I could use an outlet myself.'

So she had been right about Serena. He was not having things all his own way. Karen could appreciate the emotional frustration of loving more than one was loved; she could also understand the urge to vent that disappointment on someone or something. She herself was a thorn in his flesh, the responsibility thrust upon him through his association with her brother.

'I'd like to go home,' she said unevenly. 'There's no further reason to stay, is there?'

'There's every reason. We only just got here.' Mouth hard, he summoned a waiter with peremptory flick of a finger. 'We'll order now, then have a drink while we're waiting.'

Karen gave in, sensing the uselessness of further argument. When the menu was offered to her she shook her head, lifting her chin defiantly at the man seated opposite. 'I'll leave it to you.'

He gave the order crisply, saw the waiter depart and pressed back his chair. 'Let's dance.'

Neil saw them first, his eyes widening in obvious surprise. He said something to Barbara, then steered her closer.

'Serena here too?' he asked. 'She didn't mention it.'

'She didn't want to come.' Brad's tone discouraged further pursual of the subject. 'If you two are here alone perhaps you might like to join us?'

Neil said quickly, 'We already ordered, thanks.'

'Coffee, then. We can have it through in the bar.'

It was Barbara who answered for them both, cutting across Neil's unmasked reluctance. 'That sounds a nice idea. Shall we see you through there after we've all eaten?'

'Nice girl,' Brad commented dryly as they moved apart again. 'She might be good for him.'

'She'd also much rather be alone with him,' Karen retorted, low-toned. 'You did that purposely!'

'You're so right.' The mockery seared. 'By the time we leave you're going to be thoroughly resigned to the idea of those two together.'

'Is that what they call being cruel to be kind?' She was trembling with anger and hurt. 'You always have to know best, don't you, Brad? It wouldn't occur to you that you might be wrong! I refuse to be pushed into a situation like this just because you say so. You can order coffee for four if you like, but you'll have to drink mine as well as your own because I shan't be there!'

'You'll be there.' His hand was hard at her back, jaw clenched. 'I'll see to that.'

There was no more to be said. No use, that was, in trying to discuss the matter. Karen set her teeth against the quivering of nerve and sinew. This was one time Brad was not going to get his own way. On that she was determined.

The first roll of thunder came while they were still only halfway through the second course, sounding fairly distant but ominous. Even with the windows open to catch what breeze there was outside, and the electric fans going on fast speed above, the atmosphere was oppressive. It needed rain to cool things down, but so far there was no sign of it. Karen hoped it would continue to hold off for a while. Not that it made any difference to her plans whether it did or not. Come what may, she was not going to sit through the rest of this horrible evening making necessarily stilted conversation with two people who so obviously desired to be left alone.

That Brad was also adamant became apparent when he instructed the waiter to serve coffee and brandy through in the bar, meeting Karen's eyes with cool unflinching purpose in his own.

'Ready?'

'Yes.' She got up and accompanied him from the room, pausing in the lobby to say expressionlessly, 'I'd like to visit the powder room before we meet the others.'

'Go ahead.' He was unsmiling and aloof. 'I'll wait for you here.'

The ladies, thank goodness, was empty. Karen glanced at herself briefly in the glass, seeing the pinched look about her mouth, the darkness under her eyes. There was no opportunity to fetch her stole; hot as it was outside she would hardly have need of it. She went quickly through the side door, came out cautiously on to the terrace, and was down the steps and making her way round the side of the club-house before anyone could have noticed her.

It took her a couple of minutes to reach the road, and another five to round the bend which cut her off from sight of the club. Only then dared she slow her pace, her breathing coming fast and ragged, her limbs oddly wobbly. A brilliant flash of lightning jagging the sky ahead heralded the closest clap of thunder yet, making her shrink inside. Where she went from here she was not yet sure. Vaguely she had imagined reaching the main road, half a mile further on, then flagging down a car to take her into town where she could get a taxi. In practice that idea seemed a long way short of being a sensible one. Even if she could get a lift she might conceivably be jumping from the frying pan into the fire by accepting it.

So all right, she would walk the whole two miles into town, she told herself firmly. The tarmac was hard under her lightly clad feet but a good enough surface to make that a not impractical proposition. She thought of Brad waiting for her in the lobby, and allowed herself a certain grim satisfaction in the knowledge of his growing impatience. Eventually he would realise that she had no intention of rejoining him, but he would no doubt imagine her still somewhere in the immediate vicinity of the club. It would be half an hour at least before he could be sure she had left, and by that time she would be more than halfway home.

Lightning flashed again, revealing a landscape suddenly and totally alien. This was no English country lane; this was Africa, immense and mysterious, the roadsides dipping away into the brush and thicket which might conceivably harbour all kinds of animal life. The nearest lights were still a good quarter of a mile away, winking outposts of civilisation offering safety and reassurance if she could only reach them. Karen shivered as thunder ripped the sky apart right overhead, felt the cooling rush of wind in her face and knew the rain was coming as she had seen it come that time before, sweeping across the veld like a curtain.

The first force of it took her breath away. Within seconds she was soaked through to the skin, her hair plastered to her head and streaming. She struggled on manfully, telling herself she could get no wetter. At least in such weather any animal life would have gone to ground—or had she heard somewhere that snakes liked rain? She almost came to a full stop at that point, but common sense prodded her into movement again. Worms liked the wet; snakes were warmblooded. Anyway, even if it were true she was as likely to have one run into her as the other way round.

In the gushing torrent with thunder still rolling above, the first intimation she had of the approaching vehicle was when light washed over her, outlining her slender figure against a dark clump of trees. Then the car was drawing up beside her and Brad was leaning across to swing the door, features a grim mask.

'Get in,' he said. 'Now!'

Karen obeyed because there was nothing else to do, closing the door and huddling into her corner with the water running from her on to the seat and floor. Her skirt and blouse clung limply, the colour darkened to near black. She made no attempt to squeeze excess moisture from the material swathing her legs. Just then she couldn't find the strength.

Brad's eyes were blazing with an anger barely held in check. 'You crazy little fool!' he gritted. 'What the hell do you think you were doing?'

'Making a point.' She was starting to shiver now, despite everything she could do to try to stop it—as much from reaction as the chill of wet things. 'I told you I wouldn't let you push me into anything else!'

'Right at this moment it's more a case of where I'd like to put you!' He sounded savage, the skin stretched white about his mouth. 'If somebody hadn't seen you making off down the drive I'd still be looking for you back there. Of all the pigheaded, idiotic things to do this just about beats all!'

'Pigheadedness seems to be in vogue at present,' she came back through clenched teeth. 'Or does it come under another name when you practise it? What you tried to do was unnecessary and unfair!' Her voice wobbled dangerously on the last; she made a valiant effort to control it. 'I'm cold,' she said. 'If we have to continue this at all can we please do it after I get into some dry clothes?'

He turned without answering, reaching into the back seat and fishing up a travel rug. 'Get out of those and put this round you,' he ordered. 'You can't sit like that all the way back.' His jaw firmed afresh as he saw her expression change, the tone of his voice deepening to a real threat. 'Either you do it or I will. I'm not risking you taking a chill.'

He meant it; there was no doubting that. Karen put up a hand and began to unfasten her blouse, fumbling a little with the buttons as the wet material refused to give. 'You might at least look the other way,' she got out, and saw his lips take on the mocking slant she so detested.

'Think you deserve the consideration? You got yourself into this state in the first place. A little embarrassment is a small price to pay compared with what I'm still only a hairsbreadth away from doing to you.' His glance held hers inexorably for a moment, dropped to take in the faint tremulousness about her mouth and developed a fraction less hardness. He took out cigarettes and lit one, facing front with an ironical smile. 'Get on with it.'

It was difficult to struggle out of the clinging material within the confines of the seat, but she managed it at last, clutching the rug about her thankfully and kicking both skirt and blouse into a sodden heap in the corner. 'All right,' she said in subdued tones. 'I'm through.'

He glanced her way again, a subtle difference in his expression. 'Rub yourself dry,' he instructed briefly, and reached out to switch on the ignition as she complied, bringing the engine roaring back to life with a single jerk of his wrist.

The rain had lessened enough to make driving through it feasible if not exactly pleasant. On fast speed the wipers were just about able to cope with the flow of water down

148

the windscreen. Brad took no risks, keeping to a steady pace the whole way back to Breckonsridge. At the bungalow he took the car as close to the veranda steps as he could get it, told her to stay where she was and got out himself to come round the front and hoist her bodily indoors before she could find breath or will to protest.

In the lounge he set her on her feet again and went straight across to pour a shot of whisky, bringing it back to put the glass in her unresisting hand.

'That might help ward off any chill. You were shivering in the car.'

She was still, but not from cold. She drank some of the whisky, gasping a little as the fire hit the pit of her stomach and rebounded. She couldn't think of a solitary thing to say. If only he would go, leave her on her own. Having him here at all with her now was utterly unbearable. The rug was slipping. She clutched it fiercely to her. It was Serena she had been answering for tonight. Serena who had sparked off the need in him to hurt. That was the worst part, knowing it. Even his anger had not really been directed at her.

'Get straight in a hot bath before you go to bed,' he said now in the same abrupt tone. 'And ring through to the house first thing if you feel any ill effects at all in the morning. Do you hear?'

She nodded, unable to trust her voice, her attention rigidly on the soaked shoulders of his white dinner jacket. There was rain in his hair, clinging droplets left behind from the hand he had run through it. A will stronger than her own forced her to lift her head enough to meet his eyes, her own darkening in mute appeal. She saw a muscle contract suddenly along the line of his jaw; then she was in his arms with his mouth crushing all resistance, feeling the imprint of his fingers like steel at her back. For a long moment she was still in his grasp, wanting that kiss with everything that was in her before reaction triggered the blind searing fury which tore her free of him. It wasn't her he was kissing, it was Serena. *Serena!*

'Go away!' she blazed. 'Just go away and leave me alone, Brad! I don't want you anywhere near me!'

She didn't wait for his response, turning blindly to run from the room as if all the devils in hell were on her heels.

Morning brought no apparent after-effects of her soaking, other than a sensation of utter weariness only partially accounted for by an almost sleepless night. She got up at eight, bathed and dressed listlessly in a cotton sundress which left her back bare, then went out to toy without appetite at the toast and fruit Aaron had prepared for her.

The morning was fresh after the storm, the sun already hot but lacking the brassy glare of yesterday. She wished Keith were here—or at least, that he would get in touch. She felt totally alone, both physically and emotionally. It was like being drained of everything; even the capacity for pain. After last night Brad would not be seeking her company again. Certainly not voluntarily. She had made sure of that. Neither did she want to see him again. It was better this way in the long run.

It was gone eleven before she remembered the braai planned for today, but nothing would have persuaded her to do anything about it. For Aaron's sake alone she forced herself to eat a little of the creamed chicken at lunchtime, and felt better for it. Going without food was no solution to what ailed her. She had to shake herself up and carry on living despite everything. It would pass eventually. It had to pass. No one could go on being torn apart like this for all time. One day she would be able to look back on this period of her life and see it for what it was—a phase. Not an unimportant one, but not by any means the only vital one either. She refused to listen to the small voice that mocked her within.

She was sitting out on the veranda when Caliph came into view along the track which led through the trees towards the main house. Frozen into immobility, she watched Brad bring the stallion to a halt just below her and swing a leg over the saddle. He was wearing riding breeches and

150

boots and had a scarf tucked into the open collar of his shirt; a conventional outfit oddly at variance with the hard set of his features as he mounted the steps to where she sat.

'If I'd imagined you doing this I'd have come and got you before people started arriving,' he said. 'When you didn't contact me this morning I took it for granted you'd be over around noon. What happened?'

'You know what happened,' she said quietly and with surprising steadiness. 'It didn't occur to me that you might still be expecting me.'

'Because you got what you'd been asking for all evening?' His tone seared. 'You should be grateful you got away with as little, considering. There was more than one moment when I was on the point of ignoring the rules altogether.'

'You work to rules?' Karen lifted a deliberate eyebrow, wondering at her ability to act a part so foreign to her present emotions. 'You astonish me. I was under the impression you just made them up as you went along!'

'Let's leave it at that, shall we?' His voice was dangerous in its very softness. 'Where you're concerned my boiling point is very low. I'd hate to destroy any more of your girlish illusions.' He put a hand to his pocket and came away with two envelopes, one of them a buff colour which drew her eyes sharply. 'I collected the mail earlier. This one is for you from England,' handing over the second of the two. 'From your aunt, according to the address on the back.'

'And the other?' She was sitting upright in the chair, body tensed and expectant, making no attempt to verify his statement. 'That's a cable, isn't it?'

'Yes. And it's from Keith.' He paused, regarding her with irony. 'You'll be glad to hear he's coming back ... and bringing Denise with him. Want to read it?'

She shook her head, subsiding again until her back came to rest against the cane. 'When?' she asked.

'Monday. The afternoon flight. They'll be here before bedtime.'

Karen tried to consider the situation rationally. 'Perhaps it might be best if I asked Molly if I could stay there for a couple of days until they've settled in again. They might both feel a bit uncomfortable at first.'

'Not necessary.' Brad leaned his weight against the rail, one arm braced on the sidepost. 'You won't be here. Neither will I. I've made arrangements to take that trip up to Umfolozi, starting in the morning. We'll be away four days. Time enough for things to be back to normal when we get back.' The smile held more than a hint of a jeer. 'No, not just the two of us, honey, much as I'd jump at the chance to take you on a nature trail alone. There'll be six of us altogether; you and Serena and myself, Neil and Barbara, and last but by no means least, Ron Trent. It's more than time he had a break. The farm can manage without him for a few days. If necessary, Keith can keep an eye on things while we're away.'

Karen found her voice at last. 'I'm not going,' she said flatly.

'You are.' His tone hadn't altered, but there was a determined gleam in his eyes. 'You're going if I have to pack you out of here bound and gagged. And don't bother asking Molly if you can stay at Sunnyside because I'll make sure she understands the situation well enough to regretfully refuse. You're going to be ready and waiting, bag in hand, when I bring the car round at eight tomorrow, or I'll put you into it just as you are. Clear?'

'You make it impossible to be anything else.' It was going to be useless, she knew, but she had to make the attempt. 'Brad, please don't do this,' she begged, clamping down on her pride. 'I don't want to go to Umfolozi. Molly will be glad to have me if you don't say anything to her.'

'Sorry.' There was no regret whatsoever in his voice. 'It won't do. The others are still over at the house. Why don't you come on back with me now and join in? It would look more natural.'

'Why should you care *how* it looks?' she asked bitterly. 'So far as I'm concerned, they can all know I'm coming under protest, and welcome!'

'My God!' He looked just about at the end of his tether, fingers curling viciously about the wooden post. 'You go all out for retaliation, don't you! Can't you even try ...' He broke off, teeth coming together audibly. 'Have it your own way. I'll leave you to brood. You won't need to take much with you. Just an extra pair of slacks and a change of shirt, blouse, or whatever you like to call it. Oh, and make sure you're wearing something comfortable on your feet. We're going to be covering a fair amount of distance during the daytime.' He moved to the head of the steps, then paused. 'By the way, your things from last night are over at the house and as good as new. You can get them when we get back from Umfolozi.'

Caliph pranced skittishly when hands seized his bridle. Brad brought him under control and hoisted himself into the saddle, turning him in the same movement to head in the direction of the open veld with every appearance of a man in a hurry to be away and gone.

The day wore on and turned into evening, lamps were lit and Aaron brought through the usual fresh ice. Dinner was a simple green salad and grilled trout, followed by a crème caramel Karen barely touched. She played a couple of records from Keith's extensive collections, skimmed through the magazines she had not already seen and finally lay back and watched the clock fingers move with paralysing slowness from eight-thirty to nine o'clock. The drone of a car coming down the lane brought her to a sitting position, her tension only semi-allayed by her recognition of engine sound. Why would Neil come visiting now at this hour?

It wasn't Neil, it was Barbara. She came in hesitantly, pausing just inside the doorway to eye Karen with obvious discomfiture.

'Brad said you still weren't feeling up to scratch, so I borrowed Neil's car and came over to see if there was anything I could do,' she said. 'Do you think you'll be fit to travel tomorrow?'

'I think I'm going to have to be.' Karen conjured a smile,

waving a hand towards the opposite chair. 'I'm not ill, just tired. Is Molly going to mind you taking off like this in the middle of your visit with her?'

The other girl laughed. 'Molly is as happy as I am over the idea. She's been worried I'd find it dull up here compared with Cape Town.'

'But you don't, of course.'

'No. It's turned out to be the most marvellous time of my life.' The brown gaze was direct. 'Karen, I'm sorry if I nosed in on your friendship with Neil a bit sharply. I didn't try to push you out, it just happened so fast. I'm still trying to believe it myself. I mean ... well, you read about this sort of thing but you never imagine it could actually happen. We're both in a state of euphoria.'

'And naturally wanting to be together,' Karen said softly. 'You didn't push me out, Barbara. Neil and I were friends, yes, but that's as far as it went on either side. I'm glad for you both. I understand Neil is coming back with you to the Cape?'

'Yes, he is. I haven't said anything to the parents yet, apart from telling them I'm bringing back a friend. It's too new to spread around.'

'Will they mind?'

'What's to mind? I love Neil, and he loves me ... at least, he swears he does.' But there was no element of doubt in her voice. 'We don't plan to get married in a rush. We both want time to savour this part of our lives first. They'll like him; they can't *fail* to like him. They might be a bit dubious about our chances of sticking together initially, but they'll soon realise it isn't just a flash in the pan kind of affair. Mom was married at twenty-one herself, and she's still enough of a romantic to find that symbolic of something or other.'

'And when you do marry?' Karen asked carefully. 'Will you live at Lowlands?'

A faint cloud passed over the vivacious features. 'I don't know. We neither of us have any interest in farming as such, but unless Brad allows the twins to sell the place it seems we might have to for the time being.'

Karen glanced down at the nail she had broken earlier, feeling the sharp edge she had missed filing away. 'It mightn't be in Brad's power to let the estate be sold at all before the full term is up. Have you asked him?'

'I wouldn't dare. I quite like him, but he can be a bit overpowering at close quarters. I'd hate to cross him ... seriously, I mean. He looks just about capable of anything.'

'Yes,' Karen said without expression. 'But Neil should have it out with him himself. At least then he'd know exactly where he stands.'

'I suppose you're right. Trouble is he won't. He's relying on Serena.'

'I hope his trust won't be misplaced.' Chest tight, she added huskily, 'Would you like some coffee? Aaron is still around.'

'Thanks, but I said I'd get back. Neil is coming back to Molly's for supper, although I doubt if either of us will be able to do her justice after the dinner Brad gave us tonight. It's a pity you couldn't be there. Still, we shall have plenty of time to get together on the trail, all of us. Neil wasn't all that keen on the idea himself until I talked him round. If Brad is good enough to go to the trouble of arranging it ... to say nothing of paying for it all ... then it's hardly fair to turn it down.' She got up, stretching lithely, glanced again at Karen as she tucked the sleeveless white top back into her daffodil yellow skirt. 'Sure you'll be all right?'

'Positive.' Karen would have liked to know what Brad had said regarding Keith and Denise's absence, but there was no way in which she could ask. She went with her to the door. 'Is Brad picking everyone up in the morning?'

'No, Neil is fetching the rest of us over here and leaving his car in the garage. It's going to mean an early start. He's already grousing about that.'

'It doesn't seem to bother you very much.'

Barbara grinned. 'It's just the way men are, isn't it? Nothing is right unless they're organising it themselves. Mom always says it's best to let them do their moaning on

the principle that it's better out than in. A bit of a phil-
osopher, is my mother on the quiet; though my father is
convinced she's a total scatterbrain. He can't stand clever
women. Says they make him feel inferior.'

Karen was smiling with her involuntarily. Barbara had
that effect. Brad had been right, she was going to be good
for Neil: a fun-loving person, but one with her feet planted
firmly on the ground.

'See you in the morning,' she said. 'And thanks for calling
round. I appreciate it.'

Alone again, she listened to the departing car for a moment before turning back indoors. The letter Brad had
brought across lay where she had left it before dinner, its
pages turned to the last but one. Karen picked it up again
and re-read the lines, visualising the well loved faces of the
couple who had been almost everything to her these last fifteen years. They were looking forward to her return at the
end of the following week, Aunt Carol said. It seemed such
ages since she had gone and they could hardly wait to see
her again. She was sorry she had only managed a couple of
previous letters in reply to the ones Karen had sent, but she
had not been too well, although she was quite better now.
Friends kept asking when she was due home, and one had
actually suggested she might decide to stay on in South
Africa.

A plea for reassurance there, unless Karen was mistaken.
Well, they didn't have to worry, she wouldn't be staying.
She wasn't needed here. Not by anyone.

CHAPTER TEN

DAWN broke clear and sweet-smelling. Karen was up at first light, unable to bear the confines of her room a moment longer. A translucent glow over the eucalyptus trees heralded the sunrise. She watched the changes in the sky from the veranda, the flooding of the landscape with warmth and colour; felt the dawn breeze shift direction and die before the spreading rays. She could count on her fingers now the number of dawns she had left to experience in this part of the world. Tomorrow at this time they would be in Umfolozi. She wondered if it would feel any different out there in the wilderness.

Brad arrived promptly at eight, manner impersonal as he handed out her bag to the waiting car.

'The others should be there when we get back to the house,' he said when they were in motion. 'I want to lunch at Nongoma so we can drive up through the Nkandhala forest. Know anything about the Zulu wars?'

Karen inclined her head without looking at him. 'We touched on them at school. Wasn't it somewhere near there that Louis Napoleon was killed?'

'Close enough.' His smile was dry. 'I'd have thought Lord Chelmsford more worthy of mention, but there's no accounting for tastes. My grandfather fought at Rorke's Drift. He was one of fifty-five Europeans who survived out of nine hundred and fifty left to hold Isandhlwana. After the war he chose to settle in South Africa rather than return to England. So our origins aren't entirely alienistic, you might say.'

She was silent for a long moment, wondering why he

should bother to bring up that particular subject now, unless it was an effort on his part to dispel at least a little of the atmosphere hanging between them. They were to be in fairly close proximity for the next four days, if not exactly alone. Given any kind of leeway even small differences could become magnified a hundredfold in such conditions. What he was saying in effect was that they should both make an effort to appear on friendly terms in front of the others; to concentrate on what little they did have in common and forget the rest. She agreed with him, but it didn't make it any easier to do. What she felt for Brad was not to be forgotten, only held in cold storage for a time when she could be alone with it again.

'I left a note for Keith and Denise,' she said. 'I hope I did the right thing.'

He took up the olive branch without pause. 'Depends what you said.'

'Not a great deal. Just that I hoped they'd had a good journey, and I was looking forward to seeing them both when we get back.' She waited a moment before tagging on, 'I think you were probably right about going right away for a few days. If I'd been at Molly's, Keith would have felt obliged to come over and see me, and Denise may not have liked having to share his attention so soon.'

'She'll have to do that anyway,' he responded without expression. 'There's his job.'

'That's different.'

'Is it?' He gave her a swift glance. 'You mean a woman can share a man more easily with his work than with another person?'

'I think so, providing the job isn't more important to him than *anything* else. And Keith just proved it wasn't by risking it to go after her.'

'There was no risk attached.'

'Denise doesn't know that, though. I'm sure she'd far prefer to believe he was prepared to give up everything in order to get her back. Perhaps if she had refused to come back to Breckonsridge he might even have done it.' Her jaw felt stiff, but the words kept on coming. 'I daresay you'd find that kind of sacrifice unrealistic.'

'A shaky foundation would be nearer the mark. No matter how deeply he feels about her, any man who totally subjugates his own needs to a woman's is throwing away every atom of self-respect. And women, being the way they are, don't think much of a man who does that.'

They were already turning into the courtyard. Karen saw Neil's car apparently only a little ahead of them, for his passengers were still in the act of extricating themselves from the interior. Both Barbara and Serena were dressed as she was herself in denims and a shirt, the men in the same beige drill bush gear as worn by Brad. There was a lot of laughter and lighthearted jeering as the latter brought the estate to a stop beside them.

'Just beat you to it,' Neil said. 'Had a real job getting these females on the road, didn't we, Ron?'

'Cheek!' returned his sister in mock indignation. 'Who was it had to route our manager here out of the store sheds? If we'd waited till he considered everything in a fit state to be left we'd have got here some time tonight!'

'Only doing what I'm paid for,' came the easy reply. 'Takes a bit of getting used to this idea. Not that I'm grousing,' meeting Brad's eyes with an odd little smile. 'I daresay I'll learn to adjust once the pressure's off.'

The other man nodded back briefly. 'That's the point of the exercise. Let's get your things transferred, then Neil can garage the car and we'll be off.'

They were on their way by eight-thirty, Serena and Ron in front with Brad, the other three occupying the rear, with Karen on the right behind Brad. The eyes, glancing continuously into the mirror, seemed to look directly into hers, although it was probably an illusion. She took a studied interest in the passing scenery, joined in any general conversation but made little voluntary contribution, too vitally aware of the closeness of Serena's shoulder to the broader one at her side. It was something she was most likely going to see

159

a lot of this next few days, she reasoned hollowly, so she had better get used to it. They belonged together, those two.

Their first stop was at Gingindlovu for coffee. Retracing her steps to fetch the scarf she had left draped over the back of her chair, Karen found herself temporarily alone with Neil who had stopped behind to buy cigarettes before going out to the waiting car.

'Hi!' he said casually. 'How's things?'

Karen took up the draped scarf with a wry inward smile. When Neil lost interest he obviously did it wholesale. They might have been first-time acquaintances from the way he had spoken. One could only hope that what he felt for Barbara was of a more lasting nature.

'Things,' she said, 'are fine. Did you ever do this kind of trip in Colorado?'

'Not by car. We used to do three-day treks on horseback with blanket rolls for the hardy and tents for the rest. Can't say I think much of this going afoot business. Ten miles is a fair distance to cover in that kind of country.'

'We won't be doing that every day, though. And we'll certainly see more.'

'Depends what you want to see. Personally, I'd rather have a rhino charging the car than li'l old me! The black will have a go at anything that moves if it feels that way out.' He accepted his change from the bartender and moved with her to the door. 'Decided when you're going home yet?'

'Yes.' The word fell flatly between them. 'The end of next week.'

'I'll be in Cape Town by then. If I don't get the chance to say it before we leave, happy landings. I suppose you'll be glad to get back.'

'Yes, I will.' She could say it with conviction because in many ways it was true. Once home she could begin picking up the pieces. It was the here and now that was the difficult part.

Apart from Brad leaning on a door, the others were al-

160

ready seated in the car by the time they got outside. He watched them coming across with an expression which made Karen's face burn. Serena, she noted with a jolt, was occupying the rear seat now, leaving the one beside Brad free.

'Thought you might appreciate the change,' he said sardonically, moving to allow her access. 'Don't hang about, Neil. I want to make Nongoma for midday.'

Now it was Karen's turn to brush shoulders with the driver when they were on the move again, the knowledge keeping her stiff and tense in the seat against the movement of the car. She knew he sensed her unease by the straightened line of his mouth, but she couldn't relax. When Ron Trent began pointing out things of interest along the route she turned to him gratefully.

Eshowe was the administrative centre of Zululand, a lovely gracious little place built around the nature reserve of Dhlinza. Flowering trees lined the streets, enhancing some fine architecture and wafting scent into the air. From there to Melmoth the road ran through woodland luxuriant with sub-tropical growth and teeming with wild life. Karen was entranced and amused by the antics of the monkey packs living free in the trees, exclaiming at the exotic plumage of the bird population. It was difficult to believe that this peaceful landscape had been the scene of such bloody battles a bare hundred years ago.

She was even more transported when they left the main roadway to circle through the rolling green hills with their clusters of beehive huts dotting the gentler slopes. Here was the Africa of her imagination, where tribal life and custom still held sway; where water was drawn from a communal tap and carried proudly homewards on the heads of the graceful Zulu women; where small children played naked in the sun and ran with total unselfconsciousness to greet the intruding vehicle, one or two of the older ones putting on an impromptu display of Zulu dancing which both delighted and disquieted at the same time.

'Tourism has a lot to answer for,' was Brad's ironical

comment as he handed out candy bars from a bag under the dashboard. 'You don't want to take any photographs?'

Karen shook her head. 'I'll stick to the animals. You can't capture a whole way of life on film without giving some wrong impressions, and I'm not very good at describing attitudes.'

She almost regretted that decision when they passed a group of women happily gossiping down by a river while their washing dried in colourful array over every bush and shrub in the immediate vicinity, but she didn't think she was wrong. Impossible to portray a quality which must be both seen *and* heard on one small square of celluloid.

Lunch was a lighthearted affair, helped not inconsiderably by the two bottles of wine Brad ordered to go with the meal. From here it was only a short run down to the entrance to the reserve, so time was of relatively little importance. They had coffee on the terrace of the tiny hotel overlooking an aviary containing many different species of African birdlife. Almost inevitably there was a mynah bird caged along the terrace to beguile the visitor with its uncanny reproduction of human speech.

Karen got up after a while and went to it, cocking her head along with the sleek black one. 'Poor old boy,' she murmured. 'I'd like to let you out to stretch those wings.'

'Shut the door,' returned the bird promptly if somewhat inappropriately, then followed that with something totally unintelligible in what might have been Afrikaans before lapsing back into beady-eyed silence.

'It wouldn't appreciate the chance,' said Brad from over on her left, and Karen turned her head to find him almost within touching distance as he lit a cigarette and rested his weight against a chair back.

'Why?' she demanded.

'Because it will more than likely have been born and bred in captivity. Take it out of the environment it knows and it's lost.'

Blue eyes met grey and slid swiftly away. 'What happens

162

when we reach the Reserve? Do we start trekking right away?'

He shook his head. 'We'll make first camp by landrover the easy way. This trip is a private arrangement geared to our own needs, though we'll all be in charge of a game ranger. You'll be carrying only what you'll need during the day. The heavy stuff is taken on by car to each new stop.' His tone was even but the edge wasn't far away. 'Reassured?'

'A little.' She half turned so that she could see the others, finding them all apparently occupied with their own conversations. Serena was talking with Ron Trent, her face animated as she described something with her hands that drew a smile to his own lips. Karen wondered if she knew how the man felt about her. It seemed likely. Serena was nobody's fool. She glanced back at Brad to see how he was taking the chumminess, but he was looking at the cigarette smouldering between his fingers, cynicism in his expression.

'Maybe Barbara and Neil should come up front for a spell,' he said, and put out the cigarette between finger and thumb with an unnecessary force. 'Let's go.'

The camp at Umfolozi was situated on a hill with a superb view over the valley and the neighbouring Hluhluwe Reserve. There were comfortable cottages for the visitors with electric light laid on, ablution blocks, and a communal kitchen where each party's food was individually prepared by cooks assigned to each cottage.

'We should be staying here,' muttered Neil, obviously still reluctant to forsake all creature comforts.

Their guide for the coming few days on the trail was a Bantu named Kisani who was waiting for them alongside the hired landrover. His English was good enough for Karen to understand him with ease, although he spoke with Brad mostly in Afrikaans. They were each to carry a small rucksack bearing a day's provisions and any other small items considered essential by the individual; the rest of their stuff would be left in the car and transported out to the campsite each evening by the two men who would erect the

163

tents and cook the main meal over an open fire.

To Karen it sounded the perfect mixture of adventure and convenience. Not exactly what Brad had been referring to that night at the club when he had spoken of roughing it, but close enough for most. It said a great deal for his tolerance that he had been willing to arrange an excursion which must seem tame to him compared with previous experience, especially when considering that Serena was probably the only one among the women in the party who might have been able to take the real thing. On the other hand, he could hardly have brought her out here alone without giving that 'community mind' cause for speculation of a kind not to be lightly elicited. This was by way of a compromise; a killing of two birds with one stone, so to speak; the only way he could both look after her as he had promised Keith he would, and still spend time with Serena. To Brad Ryall there was a way round every problem. Karen wished she possessed the same aptitude for making the best of whatever circumstances presented themselves.

That first afternoon brought what was, for Karen at least, a totally new view of this land of the southern sun. The terrain itself was more open than she had anticipated, bushveld and scrub alternating with tracts of scorched grassland where the only vegetation was the flat-topped acacia tree or an occasional wild pear. Animal life at first seemed sparse to the point of non-existence. Only as the eyes became accustomed to seeking was one able to separate the real from the imagined, to follow the lines of a giraffe standing in the trees where the sun's shadows created almost identical patterns among the foliage, to catch a glimpse of a rhinoceros browsing in the brush like some relic of a long-gone age.

And then suddenly they were seeing everything, and in quantity. There were herds of wildebeeste, of nyala and zebra, the latter especially appealing in the way they would rest their heads along one another's backs to regard the passing car with quizzical expressions. Down by a stream green thornbush held no less than three white rhino, distinguishable from the black only by their squared-off lips. Brad had Kisani stop the car for a closer view, responding with a grin to the African's suggestion that they move in closer on foot for photographs.

'Anyone game?' he asked, and got the groan he deserved for the pun.

In the end it was Serena and Karen who elected to accompany him and Kisani, working their way downwind of the animals and keeping close together as they moved slowly and carefully through the thornbush. Karen's heart was beating fast, her pulse racing as if she were running hard, and yet she wasn't really afraid. There was spice in this kind of risk taking, relatively small though the danger was. The white rhino was reputedly a timid creature, far more likely to run the other way from an approaching human than charge, unless cornered. The excitement lay in seeing how near one could get before spooking them into motion.

Discovery came even as they got into a position where the girls could line up cameras for a head-on shot of the largest animal. One minute the three were browsing peacefully, the next they were crashing off through the bush with the noise and impetus of a trio of tanks, hot on the heels of the sounder of warthogs which had given the warning.

'Damn!' exclaimed Serena, ruefully lowering the poised camera. 'All I'll have got there is a blur on this setting.' She looked over to where Karen was standing a few feet away. 'How about you?'

'The same, I imagine.' Eyes sparkling, Karen was oblivious to all but the thrill of the moment, her every sense alive to her surroundings. 'Perhaps we'll have better luck next time. We *can* do it again?' she appealed, turning towards Brad on her right. 'It was great!'

He was smiling, hands in pockets as casually as if he were out for a stroll through a town park, dark hair ruffled by the breeze which heralded the approach of evening. 'We can do it again,' he agreed. 'But not today. It's time we were heading for camp.'

There were two tents already erected in the small clearing down towards the river to which they finally made their way. It was dark already when they reached the camp, but the glow of the log fire created the kind of welcome impossible to resist. Appetising smells wafted from the carcase slowly turning on a spit above the flames, overlaid by the stronger aroma of freshly made coffee.

The night air felt cool after the heat of the day. It was good to gather about the replenished fire after they had eaten, sitting on camp chairs and stools, or just on rugs laid on the ground.

Karen chose the latter, hugging her knees as she gazed into the leaping flames and savoured the feel and sound of the wilderness. There was a difference by night: a sense of being the watched rather than the watching; a stirring of primitive awareness which prickled the hairs at the nape of the neck, yet was not unenjoyable. Out there in the darkness lurked the true owners of these acres of reserve, the wild things. They themselves were the intruders.

Serena was also sitting on a rug between Brad's chair and Ron's, an elbow resting lightly along an arm of each. She had her face upturned towards the former, laughing over something he had said. In the glow from the fire she looked vital and very lovely. It was obvious that Ron thought so too from the way he watched her whenever her attention was distracted as it was now. Only when she made a move to turn towards him did he shift his eyes hastily back to the fire.

'Not still worrying about how things are back home, are you?' she asked on a note Karen privately labelled 'tongue in cheek'. 'It will be there when we get back.'

'First time I've left Lowlands for longer than half a day in almost five years,' he returned without particular inflection. 'Stands to reason I'm wondering how things are going.'

'Rather you than me,' came Neil's disgruntled voice from the far side of the fire where he was halfheartedly playing gin rummy with Barbara. 'Five years stuck on a farm. God!'

166

Karen stole a glance in Brad's direction, but his face revealed nothing of his thoughts or feelings. He was sprawling comfortably, one knee slung across the other, hands clasped behind his head supporting his neck.

'You just spent five years on a ranch,' he pointed out. 'Where's the difference?'

'Oh, there was a difference. People, for one thing. Faces were always changing. Over here the days are all the same, the faces are all the same.' The cards in his hands were still, his eyes fixed on them; only, Karen felt, for somewhere to look. 'Some of us need more scope than others. *You're* all right, Brad. You can take off when you feel like it.'

'And you can't?'

'Can't afford to.' Still his eyes didn't lift. 'Barb wants to travel too.'

Brad moved his gaze the few inches to take in her suddenly flushed face. 'You don't want a home of your own?'

'Not yet.' She was hesitant at first, then her voice gained in certainty. 'In a few years, perhaps, when I'm ready to settle down. And preferably then in a city. I'm not the country type.'

'Whither thou goest,' Serena quoted softly, looking at her brother. 'Why don't you come right out and put your cards on the table?'

'Not now.' It was Brad who spoke, his tone level but uncompromising. 'This isn't the time or the place.' He straightened, pushing the end of a fallen log further into the fire with the heel of his boot. 'Time we all turned in. We've got an early start tomorrow. You three girls going to be able to manage in one tent?'

'What's the alternative?' Serena asked blandly as she followed his example and got to her feet, and he grinned.

'None allowed.' Just for a moment his eyes found Karen's and the smile took on an edge of satire. 'The conventions must be observed.' He addressed her directly for the first time in more than an hour. 'Tired?'

She nodded, aware of Serena's shrewd study and hoping her face was as empty of expression as she was trying to make it. 'Pleasantly, though. I'm sure I'll sleep like a log.'

'Won't we all?' The mockery jarred. 'Kisani will have water heated for washing in the morning. He'll call us at five.'

'God!' said Neil again, savagely this time, and Barbara spoke to him in an undertone before drawing him away from the fire to stroll over in the direction of the women's tent and a little beyond it.

Karen said a quick goodnight to both men and went over to slide inside the tent flap. Serena followed her bare moments later, causing her to wonder if Ron had shown some lack of tact in not leaving her alone with Brad for a while. If he had it didn't appear to be worrying the older girl. She was whistling softly between her teeth as she pulled the rakishly tied scarf from her hair.

'Brad said to tell you to be sure to check your shoes before you put them on again,' she said. 'You never know what might have crawled into them during the night.'

'You must be used to this kind of thing,' Karen observed, watching the way she bent to pull back the top edge of the sleeping bag on the nearest of the three camp beds.

'Sleeping in a tent?' The blonde head shook. 'I always preferred a blanket roll.' She listened to the cry of some animal rising above the ever-present chirping of the cicadas, and laughed. 'Comforting to know there aren't any cats around, although it does take the edge off the excitement a bit too, I suppose. Wonder if we'll run across any black rhino tomorrow? Apparently the safest thing is to climb the nearest tree and stay put till it takes off again. Could be fun!' Her voice tailed off as Barbara came in through the flap, and the green eyes took on a new expression. 'Still having trouble with that brother of mine?'

'He only wants to know how he stands,' returned the other defensively, and hesitated before tagging on in a rush, 'Serena, would you object to selling Lowlands if Brad gave the go-ahead, or is Neil fighting you both?'

Brows lifting, Serena said, 'I wouldn't regard him as

168

fighting anybody. No, I wouldn't object.' A sudden little smile played about her mouth. 'Why should I?'

Why indeed? Karen turned away to start undressing. She had a feeling it was going to be a long night.

CHAPTER ELEVEN

THAT prophecy seemed doomed to come true. Long after
the other two were breathing deeply and evenly she lay
awake listening to the night noises, trying to place some of
them and succeeding with about one in ten. The sudden
whooping scream dying away to an insane giggle brought
her starting upright in the narrow bed, nerves jangling.
Neither Serena nor Barbara stirred, and after a moment she
managed to relax a little. Hyena, of course. She had read
about the animal's horrible cry but had not imagined it quite
as bad as that. When it came again she was ready for it, yet
even so it made her blood run cold.

In darkness the tent was claustrophobic. Karen thought
of the fire, the glow of which still showed faintly through
the canvas, and knew she had to get outside for a while if
she was going to sleep at all. She slid her feet slowly and
carefully out of the sleeping bag and stood up, feeling for
her shoes with her toes and sliding her feet into them in
complete forgetfulness of Brad's warning until she was
actually fastening the laces. Brogues and cotton pyjamas
made a somewhat incongruous combination, but who was
going to see them? She lifted the tent flap and stepped outside with a small breath of relief as the pressure lifted.

The fire was still burning well, only recently replenished
from the pile of logs nearby. Of Kisani and the other two
men there was no sign. Brad had said they preferred to
sleep in the car. She held out her hands to the flames, not
cold, but somehow needing the comfort, heard a sound behind her and whipped her head round to find Brad himself
standing there. He was wearing the drill slacks and had his
shirt on loose and unfastened as if donned in a hurry.

'I heard someone moving around,' he said. 'Too noisy for Kisani. The hyenas wake you?'

'Yes.' She saw no cause to tell him she had not been asleep. 'It's not a nice sound.'

'They're not a very nice animal. But necessary. All the scavengers are necessary. Without them the whole place would be one stinking hole.' He came closer to the fire himself, bending his knees to squat easily at her side. 'You shouldn't be sitting around like that. You never know what might be under you.'

'Are you telling me to move,' she asked without looking up, 'or just commenting?'

His grin was fleeting. 'If the situation were that desperate I wouldn't be wasting time talking about it. If there were any ants about you'd know it by now. At least you had the sense to put something on your feet.'

It was a bit late to feel any kind of discomfiture over her dress. Right now she had more to think about. 'What time is it?' she asked.

'Just gone midnight.' He took up a branch and stoked up the embers around the edge of the fire, the light flickering over tanned skin and turning his bared throat mahogany. 'Ten minutes and then back to bed. You're going to need some sleep even if we don't plan anything strenuous for tomorrow.'

She said softly, 'You're forcing yourself to enjoy this, aren't you? You must find it frustrating to be tied down by our capabilities instead of setting your own pace.'

He put one knee to the ground for support before answering, resting an arm along the one still raised to eye her with some expression she couldn't read. 'I didn't know it showed.'

'It doesn't. I was just guessing. We're none of us used to this kind of thing. Except Serena, of course. She seems able to adjust to anything.'

'And Neil?' The inflection was harder now. 'Would you say he was capable of adjustment?'

'No.' The moment was ripe, yet she hesitated before tak-

171

ing it, aware of the inference he would place on her interest. 'Brad, is there really no way round the terms of that trust? Neil isn't going to change. Not in twenty years, much less five! All his father did was condemn him to a decade of kicking his heels.'

'In the hope that some spark of feeling for the place might eventually ignite.' He sounded cool and clipped. 'It worked with Serena.'

Karen gave him a swift oblique glance. 'But she's more than ready to let Lowlands go. She said so earlier.'

'Only because she stands to gain more than she's losing. I've told you before, she's a different proposition. The way Neil is he'd run through his share inside a couple of years and be back here looking for more. And Serena would give it to him.'

'Even against your wishes?'

'By that time it wouldn't be anything to do with me. I relinquish all control of the situation the moment I give the go-ahead for the sale.'

'Then you *can* do it.' She was pressing too hard and she knew it, but something inside her wouldn't let her stop now. 'You could give Neil what he wants and let him go his own way, but instead you're trying to force him into a life-style he doesn't even have any aptitude for! I think you're punishing him for not being what his father wanted him to be. Making him stop here until he's served his sentence.' Her voice was impassioned. 'That's cruel, Brad!'

Eyes glittering, he said icily, 'He doesn't have to stop here. If the allowance he gets from the estate isn't enough to live on he could always get a job.'

'Doing what? He isn't trained for anything.'

'He's trained for one thing . . . eliciting support! I'll have to ask him the secret some time.'

'There is no secret. I'd feel in sympathy with anyone in his position.'

'You mean you automatically jump in to protect what you see as the underdog regardless of how badly you get bitten. It might be admirable if it weren't so sickening!' The lean

172

features were tensed, his voice low but deadly. 'I'd like to shake you till your teeth rattled, except that it would do me more good than it would you. Can't you get it into your head that he isn't worth what you're going through!'

Karen set her jaw hard. 'Barbara thinks he is.'

'That's her look-out. We're talking about *you.*'

'Not through my choice.' She came unsteadily to her feet. 'I daresay you're right and it's none of my business, only it's time somebody set the record straight where you and Neil are concerned. You despise him because he's not the man you think he should be, but why should you, or his father either, for that matter, be the one to set the standard? If you ask me, you like having the power to control other people's lives, Brad. It's called tyranny, in case you weren't aware of it!'

Grey eyes blazed as he came upright. One hand shot out and grasped her hair at the nape, pulling back her head and drawing a small gasp of pain from her lips. For a long tense moment he held her there, his wrist hard across her cheek, mouth a savage line, then he brought himself forcibly and visibly under control again. When he let her go it was with a roughness that caused her to stumble a little.

'Consider yourself lucky we're not here on our own,' he said tautly. 'Or I might just feel obliged to finish this thing once and for all. If anything, I'd say you knew less about handling people now than you did a month or so ago!' He waited, brows lifting as he studied her strained face in the firelight. 'No comebacks? Perhaps you're wise!'

'Brad ...' Her voice had a crack in it. 'I ...'

'Don't.' He was calm again but dangerous with it. 'I've had just about as much as I can take. Just do me a favour, Karen, and go on back to bed.'

She turned without attempting to speak again and made her way back across the scorched grass to the tent, lifting the flap and passing through with a spreading numbness inside her. What she had said to him just now might have held some slight element of truth, but there were ways of putting it that didn't have to include the kind of accusation

173

she had flung at him. She had wanted to hurt, she acknowledged. Something alien and frightening had taken her over during those emotive moments, driving her to rake him with claws just as ruthless as any big cat's. She loved him, yet right then she had hated him too, and with an intensity that appalled her. Was love always like this, or was it only in her to experience such wildly conflicting emotions?

Sheer exhaustion eventually claimed her mind. She awoke again when Kisani gave them the promised call, opening her eyes on a world filled with dawn shadows and the sound of a rain bird crying *it-will-rain, it-will-rain*, over and over again. Memory came springing to life like a bad dream. She sat up jerkily, summoning a smile in answer to Serena's questioning one.

'You have a restless night?' queried the other. 'I've a vague recollection of waking up and finding you gone at some point, only I must have nodded off again before I had time to get worried.'

'I only went out for a few minutes,' Karen assured her. 'I couldn't sleep at first.'

'Just the initial strangeness, I expect. You should be okay by tonight.' She was getting out of the sleeping bag as she spoke, kicking off her pyjamas and reaching for her day clothes. 'Hope you can manage with a lick and a promise so far as washing is concerned, because that's all you're likely to get out here.' She grinned. 'Unless you'd like to risk a dip in the river? The crocs probably won't mind.'

'I'll not bother finding out.' Karen leaned over and gently shook Barbara by the shoulder, well able to sympathise with the other girl's groaning reluctance to start another day. 'Breakfast in a few minutes. I can smell it cooking!'

The men were already up and about when the three of them finally emerged. Neil was sitting on one of the camp stools outside their own tent looking so pathetically resigned that Karen couldn't help smiling.

'I'd have thought you'd be accustomed to early rising,' she remarked lightly when he came over to get a mug of

174

steaming coffee from the cook by way of a start to the meal. 'Didn't you strike camp as early as this in Colorado?'

'No, we didn't,' he acknowledged. 'A civilised seven was good enough for us.'

'Over there you were after different things,' said Brad right behind them, and they both stiffened. 'Dawn and late evening are the best times to see game, but if you'd rather lie in ...' There was intolerance in the way he allowed the sentence to trail off.

Karen steeled herself to turn her head and meet the grey eyes, but they were shuttered and impregnable. The night was behind them, and there, apparently, it was going to stay.

'What time do we move out?' she made herself ask.

'As soon as we've eaten. The boys will strike camp and go back to base for the day. We'll never be more than a few miles from the main station at any time.'

'Don't say that,' Serena objected, joining them. 'It takes all the fun out of it! I'd rather believe myself a thousand miles from civilisation with only a strong male arm to save me from the savage hordes! Do you think it could be arranged?'

Brad's smile lacked spontaneity. 'There's every chance. Get some food inside you and let's get on our way.'

Serena raised expressive eyebrows at Ron Trent as the other man moved away. 'Our leader sounds fed up. Would you say we were beginning to get on his nerves?'

Ron shrugged and looked uncomfortable, his glance momentarily finding Karen's in a way which made her wonder if her conversation with Brad had been overheard last night. 'He probably just got out of bed the wrong side. We all have our off days.'

'Not you,' Serena returned on a subtly altered note. 'You're always the same. I remember thinking when Dad first took you on, now there lies a stable character!'

'Old reliable.' The irony was faint but unmistakable. 'I think we'd better eat.'

They left camp at a quarter to six with the sun already well above the horizon but not yet hot enough to have

175

driven the game back into deeper shade. A small herd of impala breakfasted among a clump of trees; brightly plumaged birds flew out of a thicket with a sudden whirring of wings to take to the cloudless blue sky. Kisani pointed out the soaring shape of a tawny eagle hunting for food, drawing a comparison with the repulsive maribou storks standing sentry in the river. Karen found it difficult to believe that once in the air such hideous creatures could match the eagle in grace of flight, but was forced to concede the point when one elected to demonstrate its redeeming feature.

They saw rhino again, but only the white. This time they managed to get some good snaps from an angle which made the animals look even closer than they actually were, before the attendant ox-pecker birds gave warning of their presence. A herd of buffalo grazing in semi-open grassland presented a far greater challenge to stalking skill. Kisani would not allow them to approach too closely. The African buffalo was unpredictable, and dangerous when aroused, their massive curling horns formidable enough in appearance to put caution into the bravest heart.

Zebra and wildebeeste herded together, the keen sight of one combining with the acute hearing of the other to form a near perfect and instinctive defence against the predators they would normally have to combat. Everything seen through Kisani's eyes took on meaning and purpose, was allocated its rightful place in the scheme of things. Only in that very lack of predators did the cycle remain incomplete. Karen for one couldn't find it in herself to regret the absence of the killer cats from the ruggedly peaceful landscape.

Lunch was a packed meal eaten in the shade of a handy clump of trees, with a choice of beer or fruit drinks by way of liquid refreshment. It was Serena who suggested splashing hot and weary feet in the ankle-deep stream running nearby, but it was only the three girls who finished up taking advantage of the opportunity. The water was refreshingly cool if a trifle muddy on the bottom. Afterwards it seemed easiest to let their skin dry off naturally in the sun before donning shoes and socks again.

Karen was tying her shoe laces when Kisani motioned them suddenly to silence, his eyes cocked towards the thicket they had skirted earlier.

'Black rhino,' he said softly. 'Cow and calf.'

The calf was hidden by thorn scrub for the moment, but they could all pick out the hulking, armour-plated shape of the mother reaching a prehensible lip for a juicy piece of foliage not a couple of hundred yards from where they stood. She looked preoccupied right now, but the leaf-shaped ears set high on her massive head would be tuned in to every unusual sound.

'We're downwind of her,' Brad observed. 'She can't scent us from there.' He took a swift glance round their immediate surroundings and appeared to come to a decision. 'Get yourselves up in the trees, you girls, if you want some close-ups. You and Neil too, Ron. We'll work round behind her and let her get wind of us. With any luck she'll come right through this way.'

'And keep right on going, I hope,' murmured Serena *sotto voce*, and drew an impatient glance.

'If it scares you say so and we'll fade out while the going's good.'

'When you bark like that I'm more scared of *you*,' she retorted dryly. 'This is supposed to be a pleasure trip, not an endurance test, isn't it?'

Karen was standing next to her. She knew it was not by accident that Brad's eyes flicked briefly in her direction before he allowed his features to relax into the satirical grin.

'I was forgetting. Do you want to photograph that rhino or not?'

'Sure.' Her tone was bland. 'Choose your perch, boys and girls.'

From the vantage point of the fork into which she scrambled, Karen found she could now see both cow and calf quite easily. They were still browsing peacefully enough, the smaller animal snuffling among the tender young shoots of new growth close in to his mother's side. She could also

177

see Brad and Kisani circling round to get behind the pair, their approach unhurried and comfortingly confident. They both looked thoroughly at home in the bush, like a couple of hunters on an old-time safari—except that the gun Kisani wielded would be used only in the direst emergency in this day and age.

The first intimation of awareness on the rhino's part came in the sudden lift of the great horned head and a radar scanning of pricked ears as the tiny eyes short-sightedly probed the source of the scent now touching the animal's nostrils. A loud snort preceded a few steps taken towards the two men hidden among the far brush, then it paused and considered a moment before apparently chang-ing its mind, wheeling instead and crashing in the opposite direction with the calf trotting obediently at its side, the pair of them heading straight for the trees where the watchers were perched.

Karen took her first shot as they came out from the main body of thorn scrub, head on to the approach. With the pocket type camera she was using, turning on the film was simply a matter of pushing a thumb slide underneath, thereby making it possible to take a whole series of pictures within a very short space of time. It was as she took the second that she heard the shout behind her. When she swung round it was to see Serena half lying, half sitting on the ground at the foot of the tree she had been sharing with Ron, full in the path of the lumbering mammals.

Whole seconds seemed to pass in frozen horror before anyone moved, although looking back on it afterwards, Karen was certain that Ron's leap from the tree to land at Serena's side must have been almost instantaneous. What he did then was the bravest thing she had ever seen, running straight towards the rhinos with wildly waving arms and shouting at the top of his voice in an endeavour to turn them aside. What he did manage to do was to stop them both dead in their tracks, the aggressive snorting of the cow mingling with the higher pitched squealing of her offspring as she weighed up this new threat. Whatever the process of reasoning possible inside that ungainly head it was evidently enough to place the safety of her calf before thoughts of vengeance, for she turned suddenly and veered off into the thorn at right angles to her point of exit, shouldering the young one ahead of her until they both vanished from sight over the lip of a rise.

Brad and Kisani arrived on the scene as they were helping Serena to her feet, having heard the shouts on route. Brad looked shaken and drawn on learning the details, running his hands over the arm she had fallen on to feel for possible breaks, despite her protests that she was only bruised and a bit jolted.

'I'm not even sure what happened,' she said in much subdued tones after he had insisted on her sitting down again for a while. 'One minute I was up there, the next I was lying down here with that big brute coming straight for me. If it hadn't been for Ron ...' She looked up at the man at Brad's side with gratefully moist eyes. 'You probably saved my life.'

'There's no probably about it.' Brad's tone was level but with an underlying seriousness that got through to them all. 'You'd have been killed if he hadn't done what he did. He could have easily have been killed himself into the bargain if that cow had attacked instead of turning off.'

Neil was pale, his features taut with something more than just shock. 'It wouldn't have happened at all if you hadn't suggested the whole damn business in the first place. If anything had happened to either of them you'd have been directly responsible!'

Brad looked at him for a long moment, strain in the line of his mouth. 'Think I don't know it?' he asked quietly. 'We're about a couple of miles from tonight's stopping place by the nearest route. I suggest we go there now and wait for the car to arrive, then spend tonight in the main camp. Give everyone's nerves time to settle before we decide whether to call the rest of the trip off or not.'

'No, please.' Serena was looking more herself again, the colour returning to her cheeks. 'I don't know about anybody else, but I want to go on with it as planned.' The smile was deliberately jaunty. 'I'll be able to dine out on this story for years. The day I was nearly trampled underfoot by a rampaging rhino!'

'Shut up!' Ron said on a rough note, then coloured up suddenly to the roots of his hair. 'I'll get our stuff down out of the tree,' he added hurriedly, and took himself off.

'Well, what do you know!' Serena's tone was a curious mixture, her glance at Brad wryly humorous. 'You didn't set this up on purpose, by any remote chance?'

The reply was brusque. 'Don't be an idiot. Like the man said, leave it alone. Are you fit to walk?'

Karen didn't wait to hear Serena's reply to that latter question. She walked a short distance off and sat down beneath the tree she had so recently vacated herself, leaning her back against the trunk and trying to still the quivering in her limbs. There was something here she didn't understand; some element which didn't quite jell. Surely most men with the knowledge of such a close brush with death for the woman they loved would have followed a blind instinct to snatch her into their arms and hold her close, if only for a moment. Brad had reacted with concern, and with obvious self-accusation, but with little sign of any deeper emotion. Or was it simply that he knew Serena would not have welcomed any show of emotion in front of the rest of them? It all seemed so odd. Even if she didn't love him the way a woman should love the man she was going to marry, she should surely have needed the comfort of a pair of strong arms about her after that experience—and whose better? Karen closed her eyes against the lowering glare of the sun as the wave of longing ran through her. When the shadow fell across her she knew instinctively who was standing there in front of her.

'If you're feeling sick put your head down between your knees,' he said.

'I'm all right.' She opened her eyes and looked up at him almost remotely, registering the drawn quality of his expression without attempting to analyse it further. 'It ... it all happened so fast.'

'I know. But it's over now, and it won't happen again.' His tone was steady and reassuring. 'If you feel you've had enough of all this, Karen, I'd rather you said so honestly, not carry on regardless just to fit in. It hasn't been a very good introduction to the Africa I wanted to show you.'

Her smile felt wobbly, but she made it stick. 'It's been a very exciting one, though I wouldn't like to do it every day. If Serena is sure she feels all right to carry on I'd like to finish this part of the course. I might never get another opportunity.'

'Serena would weather worse than this if it brought her closer to what she wants,' he said enigmatically. 'And opportunities are made, not waited for. That's a point we might all bear in mind.' He held out a hand. 'Let's have you on your feet. We have a way to go yet.'

They made the prearranged site inside the hour, predictably finding nothing there as yet. Kisani said the car should arrive at four, which gave them about thirty-five minutes to wait. He himself moved up to the nearest piece of high ground to watch for it, leaving the rest of them to their own devices. A cloud had settled over the group since the episode with the rhinoceros. From a stilted beginning conversation soon just about petered out altogether. Brad leaned against a tree trunk smoking a cigarette and viewing the distant hills with a weary cast to his features. Only when the cigarette was finally finished did he move, pushing himself upright and glancing across at Neil.

'I want to talk to you,' he said.

The other four watched the two men move away without comment. Glancing at Serena, Karen saw she was smiling to herself as if she already knew what Brad was saying to her brother. Then she looked up again and saw Neil's changed expression as he shook Brad's outstretched hand, and knew herself. Brad had told him he could go ahead and sell out. Nothing else could have wrought such a transformation. If what she had said last night had helped precipitate the decision in any way she could find no gratification in it. Neil and Barbara had their chance now; she hoped they would use it to the best advantage.

There was no disguising the former's jubilation as he came back to the group, leaving Brad where he was.

'It's in the bag,' he said to Barbara. 'He even has a buyer lined up!' He caught his sister's eye and paused. 'Did you know about it last night?' he demanded. 'Was that what all the innuendo was about?'

She shook her head. 'I wasn't that sure he'd do it. He always felt pretty strongly about keeping the Harlow name at Lowlands for Dad's sake.'

'But something he said must have made you suspect he was considering it.'

'I guess it did. He said he hoped this trip would resolve all our problems, including his own.'

'Didn't know he had any.' The grin was boyish and exuberant. 'Unless he means *you*!'

His sister gave an exasperated sigh. 'Will you get it through your thick head that Brad and I don't have anything going for us! You've been pushing us at one another since the day we got back to S.A. and we're neither of us interested. Not in any way that counts.'

'Sorry.' Neil looked nonplussed for a moment, then shrugged. 'You can't win 'em all!' He caught Barbara's hand. 'Come on, sugar, we've plans to make.'

Karen drew an unsteady breath and looked across at Ron, expecting to see him as shattered as she felt herself. But there was no sign of shock in the thin features. If anything, he looked more relaxed now than he had at any time since setting off yesterday, as though the decision had resolved something for him too.

It was only when she saw the way Serena was watching him that things began to click into place at last. Ron was the buyer Brad had in mind for Lowlands. It had to be him! And he was also the man Serena wanted. She wasn't even bothering to hide it any longer. But where did that leave Brad? He had told her he was going to marry Serena. Or had he? Her thoughts paused there. Was it she herself who had read more into what he *had* said than he had intended? She tried to think back, but it was all too confused. All she could hold on to was the one basic fact: he was not going to marry Serena now. Further than that she dared not allow herself to think at all.

He was coming towards them now, expression unrevealing of anything but the job in hand. 'The car's here,' he announced. 'No reason why we shouldn't lend the boys a hand setting up camp.' He glanced at Ron and paused, then moved his shoulders as if in wry apology. 'I decided not to wait any longer. Hope it didn't throw you.'

Serena said slowly, 'You mean you've known all along that Brad intended to let Neil sell out his share?' It was Ron she was addressing as if the other two weren't there, eyes sparking angrily. 'And you were going to let me spend four days on tenterhooks wondering how I was going to get round that blasted pride of yours if he didn't come through! Of all the ...'

Brad took hold of Karen by the elbow and drew her away from the pair of them. 'Let them sort it out between themselves from here on in. If they're going to be partners they're going to have to decide who's senior.'

She said huskily, 'I'm not sure I understand any of this. How ... long have Serena and Ron been planning to marry?'

'Let's just say that Serena realised what she'd missed most about home as soon as she saw him again, and Ron had never forgotten her. Trouble was his pride wouldn't have let him ask her to marry him while he was only the manager at Lowlands, and the only way to put him in a position where he'd feel on equal terms meant giving Neil the right to sell his half of the estate to him.' His tone was matter-of-fact. 'I had to make quite sure there was no chance of his coming to feel what his father wanted him to feel first. That's why I waited. I planned to straighten it all out on our last night in Umfolozi, but there suddenly seemed no point.'

Karen took a quick glance at his profile, registering the

hardness of line with heavy heart. 'Brad,' she said, swallowing the dryness, 'about last night. I didn't really ...'

'I think you said all there was to be said on that particular subject. You might even have had a point or two.' The hardness had not relaxed. 'Forget it. Neil has what he wants now. I hope that makes you happy.'

'For him and Barbara, yes, it does. I'm glad for the others, too.' She paused, hardly knowing how to go about finding out what she so badly needed to know but unable to just leave it like this. 'I thought *you* were going to marry Serena,' she managed at last, and he stopped short to stare at her blankly.

'Who on earth gave you that idea?'

'You did. At least ...' She broke off, aware of his changing expression and feeling the colour rising under her skin. 'It doesn't really matter now, does it.'

'It matters.' He said it quietly but with an underlying note which brought her eyes to his. For a moment he just stood there studying her, then he put an arm across her shoulders and turned her away from the direction in which they had been heading. 'Let's get out of here. There are one or two things you're going to have to explain.'

They didn't go far. Just far enough into the trees to be out of sight of the rest. A young antelope froze beside a bush for a moment, liquid eyes wide and startled, then it was gone, melting into the lengthening shadows like evening mist.

'Here will do,' Brad said, and brought her round to face him, holding her there in front of him with hands resting on her shoulders while he searched her face. 'Are you in love with Neil?' he asked.

Karen shook her head, saw his eyes suddenly blaze and felt his hands tighten as if he were about to shake her.

'Then what the devil has all this been about?' he demanded. 'Why let me ...' He broke off abruptly, catching his lower lip between his teeth. 'Have you any idea what I've been going through this last couple of weeks?' he said on a rough note. 'You deliberately led me on to believe you were unhappy over Neil. *Why*, Karen?'

'I think you know why.' Her voice was low. 'I—I had to have something. I was so sure you and Serena ...' She lifted her head to look at him. 'Remember the day we had lunch at the Albert? You said then that she would be married long before the five years was up so didn't have the same interest in selling Lowlands. I thought you meant to you.'

'And that hurt?' He was gentler now, the anger replaced by something which brought warmth curling through her. 'If I'd only realised I could have saved us both a whole lot of time and anguish. I was already more than halfway to being in love with you then, but all you could talk about was how unjust I was being to Neil.' His voice roughened again for a moment at the memory. 'If it hadn't been for Serena and Ron I'd have taken the greatest pleasure in putting paid to his schemes for as long as I possibly could; especially when he ditched you the way he did after Barbara arrived on the scene.'

'He didn't ditch me,' Karen protested. 'There was never anything like that between us, Brad. How could there be when you were all I could think about?' She was shaken and still not quite believing, looking at him with an unconscious plea in her eyes. 'Can't we sort it all out later? I don't ... I can't ...'

There was no need to say any more because he was pulling her to him, kissing her as she had ached for him to kiss her; as a man would kiss the woman he loved. When they finally drew a little way apart she was breathless and dishevelled, but radiant, loving the male strength of him, the possessiveness in his touch.

'I'd hoped bringing you out here might help us come closer together,' he said softly. 'It's been a series of misunderstandings from the start, but we're close to righting them all now. You'd better marry me soon, though, before we find anything else to get wrong.' He laughed a little. 'You know, I never imagined it could happen this fast ... though I knew you were going to be trouble the very first time I saw you!' One hand was at her cheek, his thumb brushing her mouth. 'You were so different from what I'd expected of Keith's kid sister. A blue-eyed copper-top with an astringent repartee! I could have cursed when the cable came from the Harlows, but I'd promised to be in Jo'burg to meet them when they landed.'

'Then you came back and people started talking about Serena, and I felt so mixed up,' Karen admitted. 'Especially when I still wasn't sure about you and Denise.'

'Yes,' with a sudden glint. 'I still owe you for that bit of type-casting!'

'Sorry,' she offered penitently. 'But you have to admit I did have some reason for suspecting you.'

'Only because you couldn't bring yourself to try trusting me. I know I played on Keith's need of you, but that was as much in the hope of keeping *you* here as him. Talking of need ...' He paused, expression changing a little. 'Karen, you realise I'm going to be taking you away from your aunt and uncle for good? They've had you the greater part of your life; now it's my turn. We'll both go over to see them next week when you'd have been going home anyway, but I think we should be married over here with Keith to give you away. Maybe we could fly them both out for the wedding. Do you think they'd come?'

Karen shook her head. 'I don't know, Brad. They're not great travellers.' She added slowly, 'I'm not going to pretend that it won't mean anything to me to leave them, but it isn't as though I'll never see them again. And I'd definitely want Keith to be there when ...' She stopped abruptly. 'Brad, how do you think he and Denise will take all this? I mean, I can hardly take it in myself yet.'

'Will this help?' he asked, and kissed her again with satisfying thoroughness, holding her until she pressed him away with a shaky little laugh.

'No, it doesn't help. I can't think straight at all when you do that!'

'Then stop trying.' He caught her to him again, but only to cup the back of her head in his hand and study her face.

186

'Karen, they'll have to work out their own lives. They can hardly expect others to concern themselves.'

'Isn't that a rather selfish attitude?'

'Maybe it is, but it's the only one. What we have to do is thank our lucky stars that we don't face the same problems.'

'Meaning ours will be a balanced partnership?'

He grinned. 'Providing the balance rests on the right side. Any woman who cares enough can get a man to do anything she wants him to do simply by going about it the right way. Call it pandering to the male ego, if you like, but most men need to feel they're the head of the household, even if it is only a nominal leadership.'

She gave him a bland little smile. 'I'll remember that for future reference!'

'You do,' he said, 'but it's at your own risk. Once we're married I'm liable to revert to type.'

'The type I fell in love with,' she responded softly, and felt his arms close about her in a lifetime's claim.

Send coupon today for
FREE
Harlequin Presents
Catalog

We'll send you by return mail a complete listing
of all the wonderful Harlequin Presents novels
still in stock.
Here's your chance to catch up on all the
delightful reading you may have missed
because the books are no longer available at
your favorite booksellers.
Fill in this handy order form and mail it today.

Complete and mail this coupon today!

YOU'LL L♥VE
Harlequin Magazine

*for women who
enjoy reading
fascinating stories
of exciting romance
in exotic places*

SUBSCRIBE NOW!

This is a colorful magazine especially
designed and published for the readers of
Harlequin novels.

Now you can receive your very own copy
delivered right to your home every month
throughout the year for only 75¢ an issue.

This colorful magazine is available only
through Harlequin Reader Service, so enter
your subscription now!

40 magnificent Omnibus volumes to choose from:

Essie Summers #1
Bride in Flight (#933)
Postscript to Yesterday (#1119)
Meet on My Ground (#1326)

Jean S. MacLeod
The Wolf of Heimra (#990)
Summer Island (#1314)
Slave of the Wind (#1339)

Eleanor Farnes
The Red Cliffs (#1335)
The Flight of the Swan (#1280)
Sister of the Housemaster (#975)

Susan Barrie #1
Marry a Stranger (#1034)
Rose in the Bud (#1168)
The Marriage Wheel (#1311)

Violet Winspear #1
Beloved Tyrant (#1032)
Court of the Veils (#1267)
Palace of the Peacocks (#1318)

Isobel Chace
The Saffron Sky (#1250)
A Handful of Silver (#1306)
The Damask Rose (#1334)

Joyce Dingwell #1
Will You Surrender (#1179)
A Taste for Love (#1229)
The Feel of Silk (#1342)

Sara Seale
Queen of Hearts (#1324)
Penny Plain (#1197)
Green Girl (#1045)

Jane Arbor
A Girl Named Smith (#1000)
Kingfisher Tide (#950)
The Cypress Garden (#1336)

Anne Weale
The Sea Waif (#1123)
The Feast of Sara (#1007)
Doctor in Malaya (#914)

Essie Summers #2
His Serene Miss Smith (#1093)
The Master to Tawhai (#910)
A Place Called Paradise (#1156)

Catherine Airlie
Doctor Overboard (#979)
Nobody's Child (#1258)
A Wind Sighing (#1328)

Violet Winspear #2
Bride's Dilemma (#1008)
Tender Is the Tyrant (#1208)
The Dangerous Delight (#1344)

Kathryn Blair
Doctor Westland (#954)
Battle of Love (#1038)
Flowering Wilderness (#1148)

Rosalind Brett
The Girl at White Drift (#1101)
Winds of Enchantment (#1176)
Brittle Bondage (#1319)

Rose Burghley
Man of Destiny (#960)
The Sweet Surrender (#1023)
The Bay of Moonlight (#1245)

Iris Danbury
Rendezvous in Lisbon (#1178)
Doctor at Villa Ronda (#1257)
Hotel Belvedere (#1331)

Amanda Doyle
A Change for Clancy (#1085)
Play the Tune Softly (#1116)
A Mist in Glen Torran (#1308)

Great value in Reading!
Use the handy order form

Elizabeth Hoy
Snare the Wild Heart (#992)
The Faithless One (#1104)
Be More than Dreams (#1286)

Roumelia Lane
House of the Winds (#1262)
A Summer to Love (#1280)
Sea of Zanj (#1338)

Margaret Malcolm
The Master of Normanhurst (#1028)
The Man in Homespun (#1140)
Meadowsweet (#1164)

Joyce Dingwell #2
The Timber Man (#917)
Project Sweetheart (#964)
Greenfingers Farm (#999)

Marjorie Norell
Nurse Madeline of Eden Grove (#962)
Thank You, Nurse Conway (#1097)
The Marriage of Doctor Royle (#1177)

Anne Durham
New Doctor at Northmoor (#1242)
Nurse Sally's Last Chance (#1281)
Mann of the Medical Wing (#1313)

Henrietta Reid
Reluctant Masquerade (#1380)
Hunter's Moon (#1430)
The Black Delaney (#1460)

Lucy Gillen
The Silver Fishes (#1408)
Heir to Glen Ghyll (#1450)
The Girl at Smuggler's Rest (#1533)

Anne Hampson #2
When the Bough Breaks (#1491)
Love Hath an Island (#1522)
Stars of Spring (#1551)

Essie Summers #4
No Legacy for Lindsay (#957)
No Orchids by Request (#982)
Sweet Are the Ways (#1015)

Mary Burchell #3
The Other Linding Girl (#1431)
Girl with a Challenge (#1455)
My Sister Celia (#1474)

Susan Barrie #2
Return to Tremarth (#1359)
Night of the Singing Birds (#1428)
Bride in Waiting (#1526)

Violet Winspear #4
Desert Doctor (#921)
The Viking Stranger (#1080)
The Tower of the Captive (#1111)

Essie Summers #5
Heir to Windrush Hill (#1055)
Rosalind Comes Home (#1283)
Revolt — and Virginia (#1348)

Doris E. Smith
To Sing Me Home (#1427)
Seven of Magpies (#1454)
Dear Deceiver (#1599)

Katrina Britt
Healer of Hearts (#1393)
The Fabulous Island (#1490)
A Spray of Edelweiss (#1626)

Betty Neels #2
Sister Peters in Amsterdam (#1361)
Nurse in Holland (#1385)
Blow Hot — Blow Cold (#1409)

Amanda Doyle #2
The Girl for Gillgong (#1351)
The Year at Yattabilla (#1448)
Kookaburra Dawn (#1562)